MY VEGAS GROOM

PIPER RAYNE

Cover Photo: Wander Aguiar Photography

Cover Design: By Hang Le

1st Line Editor: Joy Editing

2nd Line Editor: My Brother's Editor

Proofreader: My Brother's Editor

About My Vegas Groom

Waking up next to a stranger wearing a wedding ring was not on the itinerary.

I came to Las Vegas for a quick girl's trip, but somehow ended up a married woman. What I thought would stay in Vegas followed me back to my small town of Sunrise Bay, Alaska.

Of course, my new husband—MMA champion fighter, Logan Stone—couldn't find me alone at my house to tell me he wants to give our impromptu nuptials a shot. He has to tell me in front of my entire family and half the town.

The two of us couldn't be more opposite, but he offers me a deal I can't refuse which involves me pretending we're happily married for three months. Yeah, a lot of things can change in that short amount of time, most importantly catching feelings for a man whose lifestyle I despise.

my vegas GROOM

THE GREENES

The Greenes

Hank's Kids
Cade Greene (32)
Co-owner Truth or Dare Brewery
Fisher Greene (30)
Sheriff
Xavier Greene (28)
Pro Football Player
Adam Greene (26)
Forest Ranger
Chevelle Greene (25)
Water Boat Tourist

Marla's Kids
Jed Greene (32)
Co-owner of Truth or Dare Brewery
Nikki Greene (29)
Radio Host
Mandi Greene (27)

Owner of SunBay Inn
Posey Greene (23)
Owner of Fringe

<u>**Hank and Marla's Kid**</u>
Rylan Greene (12)

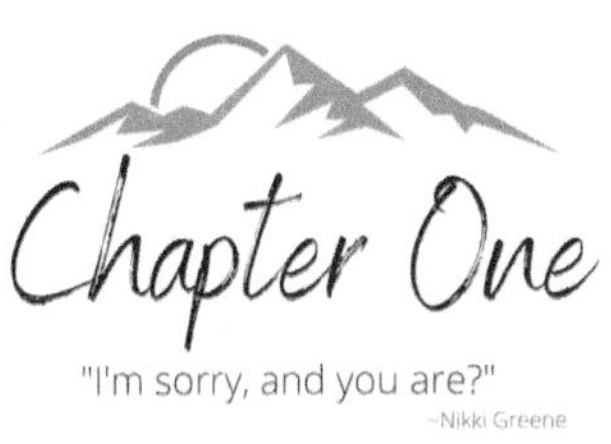

Chapter One

Nikki

I roll over on the Egyptian cotton sheets and plush mattress, my bladder screaming to release the abundance of alcohol I must've drank last night. I assume that's what happened, given the fact that my tongue is stuck to the roof of my mouth as if I ate a cotton ball.

I hear the sound of running water coming from the bathroom. I cannot believe Molly is up before me. I usually have to drag her out of bed.

Pulling the covers off of my body, I slide from the bed and tiptoe through the dark room. I trip on some clothes, but catch myself before I plummet to the floor. Seriously, what did we do last night?

I walk into the bathroom, thankful Molly's chosen not to turn on the lights because my brain could not take it right now. Plus, I really don't want to see what I look like.

Molly's been my best friend since we were young and it's not like I've never peed in front of her, so I drop my boxer shorts and sit on the toilet, groaning from the pounding in my head.

Molly's suggestion of an impromptu girls' trip to Las Vegas was a great idea. I needed to get out of our small town of Sunrise Bay. Especially since two of my stepbrothers have recently found love. Well, Adam's was found again, but seriously, whoever thought that skeptic Cade would fall in love? Sure as hell not me, even if he has a soft side. Now all heads are turned in my direction because I'm the oldest daughter in the Greene family. Everyone thinks I should want a family and kids and all that shit, and do I? Truth is, I don't know. Having Jeff Greene as your dad has a way of fucking you up where white picket fences are concerned.

Molly and I were having fun on our trip until she dragged me to that ridiculous MMA fight last night. We watched two men beat the crap out of each other for fun. I tried to humor her, but it's barbaric.

Finally, I release my bladder and it feels so good. "How on Earth are you up this early in the morning?"

Molly doesn't answer right away, but I hear the water turn off.

"I'm so hungover," I say. "Please tell me you want to go grab a greasy breakfast downstairs?"

"Whatever you want," a deep voice says.

Not the soft, giggly voice of my best friend.

I can't even process that before the shower door opens and a naked man with tattoos sprinkled all over his body of bulging muscles steps out. I can make him out from the glow of the night light on the counter. He looks vaguely familiar, but I can't place him. Was he with Molly last night? Oh shit, I shouldn't be seeing him naked.

"I hope I didn't wake you. I just had to get all that crap

from last night off and a shower always makes me feel better."

"I'm sorry, and you are?"

He chuckles. "Your husband, of course."

He grabs a towel off of the rack next to the shower and wraps it around his waist, but I'm still sitting on the toilet, mouth agape, staring at him.

But I glance at my left hand and find a sizable rock there. Meaning he's telling the truth. I am his wife. And now another Vegas statistic.

And I'm peeing in front of my new husband—who's also a stranger. He must realize my shock and horror at the same time I do because he chuckles and repositions the towel around his waist while water drips down his chiseled abs and body made of steel. It's only then that I notice some bruising on his rib cage and the side of his jaw.

"The fighter," I whisper.

He winks.

He's one of the fighters from last night. The guy who was beating the shit out of the other guy in that ring. There was kicking and punching and blood everywhere. It was the goriest thing I'd ever witnessed, and I hated every second of it. But Molly loves MMA and managed to get last-minute tickets for us, so I wasn't gonna disappoint her. Then again, I didn't know she'd gotten front row seats. While she was cheering the whole time, I mostly sat in disbelief that people found amusement in watching someone get beaten to a bloody pulp.

"After watching you throw up last night, this is nothing." He motions to where I'm still sitting on the toilet.

My face feels as if it's beet red. I threw up in front of him and now I'm peeing in front of him? My God, what else did I do?

He doesn't miss a beat, continuing on with the conversation. "So I got a call from my manager."

"Manager?" At this point, I'm not sure if I should just stand up and assemble myself or continue to sit while he carries on a conversation.

"Turns out we weren't exactly discreet with our marriage vows last night." He turns on the light.

I squint as the feeling of being stabbed through both irises assaults me. I hurry up and wipe, flush, and pull up... his boxers and his T-shirt that I'm wearing. Great.

That means I'm in his hotel room. How the hell do I get to my own hotel room and escape this situation before things get worse?

He leans his hip against the bathroom counter, his toothbrush in his hand and squirting toothpaste on it. "I had the concierge bring us up some toiletries, you know, since you used my toothbrush last night."

"I used your toothbrush?" The slight whine in my voice doesn't surprise me. I'd like someone to lock me in a closet somewhere and not let me out until I agree to behave myself like my mom taught me.

"Don't be embarrassed. It's all good. I'm cool with it."

"That's wonderful. I'm glad my embarrassment doesn't bother you, but it bothers me. Just so you know..."

"Yeah." He chuckles. "Surprised me too when I woke up this morning and remembered, but you know..." He shrugs.

What is he talking about? There's no way he's considering staying married. He obviously married a very different Nikki Greene than the one he woke up to this morning.

"I think we need to talk about this. Maybe once you have some clothes on." I wash my hands quickly because I cannot breathe in this sauna of a bathroom with him wearing a towel.

"It's cool. We can talk like this."

Sure, I'd be okay talking like that if I didn't have an ounce of body fat on me too.

"I think we'll wait because I'm... yeah... I just need to get some air." I walk out of the bathroom.

A second later, he's behind me with some remote control thing that opens all the curtains in the room to a view of the Vegas Strip in the daylight. I squint my eyes at the stabbing pain that assaults them from the light until I get used to it and then I gaze out the window.

The magnificent view is another clear sign that this is definitely *not* the room Molly and I booked. My friend and I are staying in a standard two double beds room, and this is a suite with living room couches and flat screens and a full bar. Where the hell is Molly and how did she let me get this far gone?

"I sense you might be freaking out?" he says.

I spot a picture of him and me with an Elvis impersonator between us. Won't Mom and Dad be proud? I can't even imagine what my dad would say. Then again, I don't really care. I hate that asshole anyway.

In the picture, I'm wearing a white gown that looks too small and he's wearing a blue tuxedo jacket. We're both smiling and clearly drunk. Isn't that illegal?

I pick up the picture. "You were serious about the whole marriage thing."

"Yep, we're married."

"Can we get an annulment?" I look at him.

His expression falls like someone who bet their last dollar at the slots and spun garbage. "Well, clearly we got married on a whim."

Okay, so he does have some reservations about this whole thing. Good.

"Yeah, I can't imagine you're happy about this."

He shrugs.

What's with the mixed signals?

"I don't really believe in marriage," I confess. I raise my hand as if I'm at an AA meeting. "Daddy issues."

"You don't believe in marriage?" He says it as though every girl dreams of marrying her soul mate someday. And maybe that's true—until you find your dad cheating on your mom.

"No offense, but just looking at you, I'd say you're not exactly the poster boy for marriage."

His expression dims for a split second before he grins. "Don't let the exterior fool you. I have a beating heart inside my chest and everything."

I shake my head. This has got to be a dream. Tell me this is a dream. I want to pinch myself, but I've already embarrassed myself enough what with the peeing, throwing up, and using his toothbrush, and now I'm standing here in his underwear and T-shirt.

He's still shirtless and sitting on the edge of the bed, his towel inching open farther and farther as his thighs part. Pretty soon I'll see his package, but what does that matter? I'm sure we had sex to consummate our marriage last night.

He laughs as though he can hear the hamster wheel in my head.

I bury my head in my hands and groan.

"It's all good," he says.

"It's all good?" I clench my fists at my sides. "I don't marry strangers. I sure as hell don't marry people who think it's fun to beat the crap out of people for a living."

"I don't think we should discuss my profession at this point."

He's so calm, I want to scream and see if that grabs his attention.

"You must have people who handle these things?"

He tilts his head. "People?"

"Someone who can manage us ending this."

"You're serious? Don't you think there's a reason why you married me?"

"I think the reason is tequila. That, and you looking the way you do. I probably thought you just wanted to have a good time."

He finally stands and, Jesus, that towel is barely hanging on.

"I mean, we're strangers," I add. "We got drunk and got married. It's ridiculous and we need to end it."

Based on his expression, I offended him in some kind of way. How can he not be on the same page as me? Surely he has more to lose than I do. He has a high-profile career, his reputation, and his money.

He says, "I need to go down and see my manager. He wants to talk about this marriage thing. Do you wanna come?"

We clearly have different views on what needs to happen next. I need to get him out of this room so I can leave, meet up with Molly, and we can head back home to Alaska. Hopefully this will all just go away like waking up from a nightmare.

"No, I think I'm gonna shower and get ready." I try to keep my voice even and not give my thoughts away.

"I'll bring you back some coffee. How do you like your coffee, by the way? I should know this, given that you're my wife, but I promise you'll only have to tell me once and I'll remember forever." He grins at me, and oh yeah. I see exactly why I might've thought getting married on a whim to this good guy was a good idea.

"Black and one sugar."

"Great. I'll be back soon."

He puts on a pair of low-slung jeans, a T-shirt, slides, and a sweatshirt. I could've married much worse. The man is an Adonis. He doesn't bother styling his hair that's blonder at the tips or shaving.

He walks toward me as if he's actually going to kiss me goodbye, but he stops short—probably from the look of shock and horror on my face. "I'm gonna give you some time to let this all sink in. I'll be back with some coffee and pastries and we'll talk some more."

"All right."

"Don't go anywhere." He cracks a smile. It's a great smile for a guy who's probably had his teeth knocked out more than once.

"I won't go anywhere." I cross my fingers behind my back.

"Okay, I'll be back in a little bit." He's out the door, and I finally release the breath it feels as if I've been holding the entire morning.

I sink into a chair, my limbs weak, as panic really sets in.

I married a complete stranger. Well, maybe not a *complete* stranger. Molly probably knows every fact and statistic there is to know about his fights. And my brothers were super excited when we told them we were going to the fight, so they probably know about him too. But to me, Logan Stone is a stranger. I don't know anything about him except for one small thing—he's my husband.

Chapter Two

Logan

Leaving my new bride in my hotel room isn't ideal, but Vince wasn't exactly understanding when I told him I had to shower before I'd meet him downstairs in the café, but my hangover necessitated a shower first. Making him wait any longer while I tried to convince Nikki to join us wasn't gonna fly.

Vince has managed my career forever, and he's done a bang up job. He's a big reason why I'm at where I'm at in my career. The reason I can stay in penthouse suites and invite pretty girls like Nikki to join me after fights. I don't do it that much anymore but there was something about Nikki and her disinterest in the spectacle taking place after I won that intrigued me and I couldn't resist.

When I was young, stupid, and new to success, I'd invite them all to party after a big fight, but now the appeal is lost on me. I'm a professional MMA fighter. The best in my field. Success as a fighter has allowed me to support myself, get my mom out of working three jobs, and that's enough for me. Besides, those women I used to take back to my hotel room weren't looking for love—at least not *real* love.

My mom says I'm an old soul. Not sure what that has to do with choosing not to hook up with random girls, but she insists it does.

The party girls just want to say they had me in their bed and gossip about what I was like. Or worse, snap a picture of me. They want everything that comes with stardom without anything that has to do with real feelings.

But Nikki was different last night. Maybe that's why I feel in my gut like there's a reason we got married. That's the reason I want to pursue this. Vince will surely have a coronary when I tell him I'm not gonna try to get out of this. He's gonna think I'm crazy—just like Nikki did. But I gotta say, I don't think I'm prepared to let her go so quick.

Vince is already at the café, his knee bouncing so fast you'd think he just took a loan from a loan shark and lost it all. His fingers tap on the table while he waits. He's probably on his fourth espresso of the day.

Some other managers have tried to steer me away from Vince over the years, saying he doesn't have my best interests in mind, but he's from the neighborhood I grew up in. He understands me in a way very few could, but he's also made me a rich man. And now that I've reached the pinnacle of my career, I'm not going to just get rid of him.

Then again, I've made him rich too and now I'm late in my career. Injuries take longer to recover from. Plus, the excitement is fading between every fight. Vince reminds me I need to continue doing this for my mom and although retirement sounds nice, what the hell would I do with my life? It's not like I have something else to fill my time.

He waves as I approach like I don't see him. Sitting down across from him, I spot the phone and iPad already out in front of him, ready to show me what the gossip sites are saying about my nuptials. Some photographer likely made a killing after their late-night spying gig.

When the waitress comes over, I place a to-go order for my own coffee and then Nikki's, black with sugar.

My addition earns me an eyebrow raise from Vince. "You don't take sugar in your coffee."

"Yeah, I'm aware."

He releases a deep breath, surely annoyed that I didn't just tell him who the coffee is for. But he must figure it out for himself and glean my intention from the act because he rakes his fingers through his hair. "You can't be serious about this."

"Serious about?"

"Don't play dumb, Logan."

I suppress a smile at getting him riled up. "Are you talking about me getting married?"

"Yes, marrying a girl you don't even know. Some girl you asked to join you in your room last night and spent the entire night on the balcony with. I understand that she might seem different right now and I get that you're attracted to her, but this is not some fairy tale. She's just like all the other girls. Though maybe a tad smarter since she got you to marry her."

I'm not a household name. Unless you're hanging around the Vegas MMA fighting ring or watching late-night pay-per-views, then maybe you know me. But sometimes Vince acts as if I'm an A-list celebrity.

"Honest to God, she isn't impressed by my name." I'd tell Vince that she's the one who brought up getting an annulment, but that'd make me look pathetic.

"If you want to proceed with being ignorant, then fine, go ahead, but I can tell you you're wrong. I guarantee she knows how much you're worth, and she sure as shit knows more about you than you know about her."

I shrug. "Regardless, I've decided I'm gonna stay married."

His fist clenches so hard around his espresso cup, I fear it will shatter. "You've got to be shitting me. You cannot stay married to this woman. She's going to take you for everything you're worth."

"Well, then that will be my problem, not yours." Vince might handle my career but I'm a grown man and I don't need him managing my personal life, too.

"She's obviously done something to get you to marry her. I feel like I woke up inside some movie studio's latest production or some shit like that." He finishes his espresso and raises his hand for the waitress's attention. The last thing he needs is another espresso though.

"I can't say I wasn't shocked I did it. I realize it's not something I'd normally do."

"You do realize that a large part of your fan base is women, right? And they like that you're single because they think they have a chance at being the lucky girl to score with you."

The waitress brings over his new espresso and my two coffees.

I raise my hand to stop him before he gets started again. "I think there's a reason why I did it and I want to pursue it, see what happens."

He stares at me over the rim of his drink as though I'm an alien from another planet that just came to sit across from him. "You're really serious?"

"Yes."

He shakes his head. "I think that little vacation with your mom has made you believe in all her astrological crap."

"What are you talking about?"

He waves. "You know what I mean."

"I don't." I lean back and cross my arms, tilting my head. If any woman puts me on the defensive, it's my mom. She raised me on her own, and I wasn't exactly an honor roll student. But she always had my back, and I'll always have hers.

"I think you need to end this marriage as quickly as it happened. If you let it stand, you'll never get an annulment, then you'll be sorry when you're divorcing and she's taking half of everything," Vince says.

"I already know your thoughts and I don't agree." I pick up the to-go coffees and stand. This conversation with Vince is going nowhere fast, so I might as well head back up to the room and get things sorted with Nikki. "I'll talk to you after I figure things out with her."

"Did you see the pictures?" Vince holds up his phone in front of me.

I set the coffees back down and lean in to get a better look. The picture is almost the same as the one we bought from the chapel. "Yeah, I look pretty wasted."

He scrolls to another picture that shows the ring I purchased for her. "You called in a favor at the concierge, and they called a jeweler to open up the store in the hotel. From what I hear, you had her pick whatever one she wanted and surprise, surprise—she picked the most expensive ring in the place." His hands go up in a dramatic wave as though that proves Nikki is the kind of person he thinks she is.

"I don't remember that part of it, but I can afford it and newsflash—if I'd been sober, I would've insisted my wife-to-be get the biggest rock in the place anyway." My wife deserves a sizable rock on her finger. I take my two coffees. "I want to see what's gonna happen with us."

"Fine, call me when this blows up in your face—because it's going to and you're gonna look like a schmuck. She's playing you."

If I wasn't holding these coffees, I'd grab his shirt collar and throw him up against the wall. "It's my life and I'll live it how I want."

Instead of sticking around to listen to him say more of the same, I walk away to the bank of elevators.

Nikki is my wife now. I just have to convince her to give me a chance to prove to her what a great husband I can be.

But Vince's words about how I spent a shit-ton of money on a ring and how she's gonna end up breaking my heart swim around in my head on the ride up. The last thing I want is the press thinking I'm weak.

But like my mom says, things happen for a reason. I can't deny my gut is telling me that I didn't marry her for fun and because I was drunk. There's something more.

I swipe my key card in the penthouse door and realize right away that it's way too quiet in here. I scour the entire suite and, to my frustration, come up empty. My new wife has already left me.

Chapter Three

Nikki

Swiping my key, I hurry into the hotel room I'm sharing with Molly, then slam the door and bend over to catch my breath.

"Molly!"

She comes out of the bathroom wearing a T-shirt and shorts, her hair wet from the shower. I rush to grab all my discarded clothes sprinkled over the floor and furniture from us trying on items last night and toss them in my suitcase.

"What's going on?" She sits on her bed, crossing her legs, and dries her hair with the towel. "Oh, I want details about pretty boy."

"Pack your stuff. We need to take an earlier flight. I'll explain on the way to the airport."

"What? You want to leave early? At least give me something then," she whines.

My head falls back, and I finally release a breath. I can't

keep this to myself. "Turns out pretty boy is now my husband."

Her mouth falls open and she stares at me.

"Yeah, guess I'm Mrs. Logan Stone now." I hold up my left hand although I left the ring at his penthouse.

"Isn't there supposed to be a ring?" she asks, pointing at my finger.

I walk over to my bed and flop down face-first with a groan.

Molly laughs. "Nice joke, but you just missed April Fool's Day." She shifts to get up.

"I'm serious, Mol, I married him last night," I mumble into the sheets.

"No way." I know my best friend well enough to know that she now believes me, but she still can't one-hundred percent believe I'd do something like this.

"Yes." I flip over and stare at the ceiling. "I let some man in blue suede shoes marry me to a complete stranger." I throw my arm over my face.

This happens to *other* people. People I report about on my gossip radio show in my small town. Now, if anyone gets wind of this, they're all going to be pointing fingers at me and telling me how they told me one day karma would bite me in the ass. I'm sure my stepbrother Cade will be the first in line.

"Okay, I want all the details and I want them now." Molly lies down next to me on my bed. "You cannot leave me hanging."

"If I could remember, I'd tell you, but the problem is I barely remember anything."

She nudges me. "You're such a liar. I can't believe you're holding out on me."

I hold up my hand. "I swear."

Her smile dims because just like I know when she lies—she scratches her nose with her pointer finger—she knows when I'm speaking untruths. "I never would've thought it'd be you."

"Right? I'm supposed to be in your spot, and you're supposed to be in mine."

"Whoa, now." Molly's forehead crinkles.

"You're the wild one. The one who believes in love and marriage and happily ever after. I don't want to ever get married."

"Well, too late for that."

"It's like we're in some *Freaky Friday* revamp where we switched places. I don't do things like this." My voice grows louder because no matter what, everyone in my family will find out about this and I'm going to be razzed for the rest of my life.

"If only." She pinches me.

I bring my arm closer to me. "Ouch!"

"Yep, we're still in reality." She smiles and nudges me with her toe. "Stop beating yourself up. So what? You married a hot stranger. Could be worse. You'll get it annulled and no one will ever know. You're not the first and you won't be the last."

"That's the worst part. I'm not sure he wants to end the marriage." I sit up but bury my head in my hands.

"Hate to bring this up now, but where is your hubby?"

I groan at her pet name for a man I only know as someone who beats people up as a career choice. "He went to talk to his manager and get me a coffee."

"And yet you're here."

I give her a look.

She sighs. "You shouldn't let your parents' divorce dictate your feelings about this."

I'm the first to admit I have trust issues because of my father cheating on my mom. But that's what happens when the first man you love falls so far down from the pedestal you placed him on. You tend to think every man is going to follow.

I peek at her through my fingers. "Right, because marrying a public figure like Logan would be great for me with all my issues. I mean, the women hanging off of him all the time, temptation at every turn. I might as well just reserve my spot in therapy now."

"Maybe you should give this a shot. He seems like a sweet guy. You're being way too hard on him. I went out to the balcony a few times and you guys never even noticed me, you were so enraptured with one another."

I lock eyes with her for a moment. She's right. Remembering the earlier part of the night, I recall that he really is a great conversationalist. And then another memory hits.

"*Ugh!*" I bury my head in my hands, wishing I could pull out my hair.

"What?" Molly asks, but there's a hint of humor in her tone.

"I told him I want to start a podcast," I whine. "I think I asked him to be on it."

She laughs and runs her hand down my shoulder and upper arm. "Relax. The man married you. Being on your podcast is just part of his husbandly duties."

I can't believe I told a complete stranger about my dream of interviewing celebrities so they can tell their truth and reveal different sides of themselves. I haven't even told most of my family. My face feels as if I fell asleep in the desert for three days. "Molly, I need to go home."

"Running away won't make this go away. I think you should deal with this now."

I get up off the bed. "No way. He can send divorce papers up to Alaska. I'll sign them and that will be that."

She sits on the bed, not moving, looking at me as though I'm crazy.

"Come on. Let's get to the airport."

"But our flight isn't until late tonight. I want to gamble a bit before we leave."

I shake my head. "We need to get to the airport and get on an earlier flight."

"So you marry a stranger and it cuts our girls' trip short?" She stands and heads over to her suitcase.

"Well, you should've been there to stop me. Where were you last night anyway?"

She raises her eyebrows and shrugs. "One minute you were on the balcony and the next you were gone. I called you and you answered sounding happy. Said you were out having fun with Logan and you'd see me in the morning."

She folds her clothes while I opt to go with the panicked toss-them-in-the-suitcase route. Who cares about wrinkles at a time like this? All I can think of is what my mom will say when she finds out. No matter what, I have to keep this news as quiet as possible.

Molly's phone pings and she takes a break from packing to sit on the bed and scroll through her phone. "You could've married worse, that's for sure."

"There will be plenty of time to look at your phone after we're at the airport." I zip my suitcase and head to the bathroom.

"Are you sure you don't want to shower? I mean, you smell a little like a brothel."

I stop short and stare at her. She laughs and holds up her hands.

"I don't even want to know how you know what a brothel

smells like." I go into the bathroom to brush my teeth and wash my face at least.

Standing in front of the mirror, I look at my reflection. Black mascara is smudged around my eyes and my hair is stringy and dirty. Molly's right that I should clean up, but I'm fairly sure if I stick around Vegas, Logan will find me.

Once I'm safe and sound in Alaska, I can reach out to him or his people and get the divorce or annulment going. By then he'll have come to his senses and seen that he was drunk and really doesn't want anything to do with some small-town girl who despises what he does for a living.

Partially groomed, I walk out of the bathroom with my toiletries in hand. "Better?"

She doesn't laugh and doesn't crack a smile. Her gaze rises from the phone, and she hands it over. "Maybe we should stop and get a hat for you on the way to the airport?"

The first thing I notice on her phone is the picture of Logan and me walking out of the chapel. Then another picture of the ring, and another of us at the chapel with Elvis between us. "I look horrendous."

"You look pretty. I mean, pretty drunk, but gorgeous." Molly smiles. "But if it's on the gossip mill sites, you can bet..."

My stomach drops. "Marla already knows."

My love for celebrity gossip comes from my mom. I remember from a young age that instead of reading the newspaper every morning, my mom dove into the online gossip sites. It's her one and only vice, though she'll deny it if you ever ask her.

"Let's get you home and showered and prepped with answers for Marla."

I stare at the picture of Logan and me. He really is a good-looking guy. My stomach stirs with butterflies, but I shake my head because men like him aren't the ones you settle down with. I told myself a long time ago if I ever got married, it would be to a quiet man who was the complete opposite of my father. And Logan sure as hell isn't that man.

Right now, I can't worry about Logan. I need to worry about dodging my mom until I can figure this all out. So I need to go make an appearance at my brothers' brewery and get out of there before she shows up.

Chapter Four

Logan

I'm sitting on the couch in the hotel suite, staring at the wedding ring Nikki left behind.

I should've known she'd run. She didn't seem all that into me when she woke up this morning. Actually, she seemed frightened of me and what we'd done.

I guess I shouldn't expect her to be on board with being married to a stranger. The fact that I'm cool with it is probably because I was raised by a woman who believes in signs. Or maybe it's that the fighting doesn't thrill me like it once did. I feel like I'm coming up on the time to conquer something else in my life. Maybe that's marriage.

My phone vibrates in my pocket and I pull it out to see my mom's name across the top.

I sigh. Might as well get this over with. "Hey, Mom."

"Is it true?" My mom has that tone that says she wants all the juicy details. She keeps up with my career extensively.

"How's the weather in Florida?" I ask, laughing.

"Weather? Come on. Don't make me beg." The lightness in her tone helps alleviate some of the despair I felt when I returned to an empty hotel room.

"I have no idea what you're talking about."

"Then put my daughter-in-law on the phone and I'll ask her." She laughs.

I shake my head, staring through the huge windows at the skyline of Las Vegas. A view like that should make me feel as though I'm on top of the world, and at one point, it did. Not so much lately. Right now, all I envision is Nikki pressed up against the glass last night when we got back from the chapel. That one memory from last night feels more like a nightmare now, knowing I'll never be able to experience it again.

It doesn't seem fair that I have to sit here in this room and relive what we did when she gets to disappear.

"Turns out your daughter-in-law isn't so fond of being a Stone."

Out of everyone in my life, my mom has been there for me and always been the one I could confide in. When I started to fight at school, she's the one who picked me up from the police station and urged me to put my fists to productive use to channel my anger at my father. And she's the one who saw the good in me when so many others only saw the bad.

"I know I'm biased, but any woman would be, or should be, thrilled to be Mrs. Logan Stone."

I frown. "Turns out, not her."

She sighs, and I hear the spoon swirling in her tea mug. "And what are you gonna do about that?"

"What can I do about it? I can't lock her up or chain her to the bed." I refrain from telling my mom that I asked her to stay. That would only make me sound pathetic, and I like that my mom thinks I'm a perfect guy.

"Well, what was it about her that made you marry her?"

"Other than the shots of tequila, you mean?" I don't pause long enough for her to respond. "But I know where you're going with this and I'm gonna tell you that yeah, I do think it's a sign."

A sigh of contentment flows through the receiver. "I know you've been struggling with your decision about retirement. This isn't about you finding another thrill since fighting doesn't do it anymore, is it?"

That's the problem with my mom. She can pretty much sense everything that's wrong with me and isn't afraid to call me on my shit. She knows me better than anyone.

"I haven't even decided about retirement. Vince will kill me if I retire anyway. I think the whole marrying a stranger thing... well, I wish I could figure out the reason why I did it."

"Why? Log, I taught you never to ask why. What is, just is."

That's my mom. She believes in gut feelings—always has. She thinks we all have a path in life that's already set out in front of us. So I know she probably believes that Nikki was brought into my life and I married her on a whim because I was meant to.

"I'm not really into chasing things that don't wanna be caught."

She slurps her tea. "Who said she doesn't wanna be caught? Did she?"

"Her actions spoke louder than her words."

"You know, I've seen you do a lot of fighting in your days." She pauses as if she's trying to be dramatic. "I'm not talking about just in the ring."

I know what she means. Sometimes I feel as though I've been fighting for everything I've ever gotten my entire life.

"Say what you want and let's just get on with this conversation," I grumble.

"I love you, sweetie. You're my little boy. But you're as bullheaded as those bulls in the rodeo. Actually, you're as stubborn as those stupid men who ride the bulls."

"Gee, thanks, Mom." Usually she's much more complimentary of me.

"I know when your dad left us what that did to you."

"I'd rather not talk about him right now. He has nothing to do with what's happening."

She scoffs. "Are you kidding me? He has everything to do with what's going on. So she ran? I can't imagine finding out that I married a stranger in Vegas. If she was sitting in bed with you right now, I'd probably be skeptical of her and her intentions with my baby boy."

I didn't imagine that my mom's advice would actually make sense. Usually her advice is more along the lines of 'listen to your gut, the universe is working for you, not against you, this crystal will bring you healing.'

"The fact that she's not there with you now and that she thinks that becoming your wife might've been a bad decision says she might just be the girl for you." Another slurp of her tea.

"Seriously? You think she's the girl for me *because* she doesn't want to be with me?" Maybe I was wrong. Maybe my mom has lost it.

"If the girl had stuck around, she would've been with you for the wrong reasons. I see those girls when I go to your fights. The ones who hang off you and try to use their bodies to sway you into doing their bidding. You need someone who's going to challenge you."

My mom is right. Something about talking with Nikki last night stirred something deep inside me. I have a vague memory of us talking on the balcony before too many drinks blur the rest of the night, but I do remember enjoying myself for the first time in a long time. And the fact that she never backed down about hating my profession, telling me how barbaric it was, was a total turn-on and shows she won't cater to whatever I say.

"What do you expect me to do?" I ask my mom.

"Well, surely you know her name."

Yeah, and the fact that she lives in Alaska. Who lives in Alaska besides moose and bear?

"Yeah, it's Nikki Greene."

"Nikki—I like it. And where is my daughter-in-law from?"

I lean back into the couch and push a hand through my hair. "A small town in Alaska."

She laughs. "Alaska?"

"Yep."

"I've never been to Alaska." Here we go. She's going to try to swindle me into bringing her if I decide to go up there.

"What do you expect me to do? Am I supposed to go up there and get on my knees and beg her to stay married to me?" Just the thought of me showing up in her town and having the press discover it, only to return home alone... just no. Who the hell wants their heartbroken face all over every media page?

"I don't think that's such a bad idea."

"I'm Logan Stone. Why on Earth should I beg a practical stranger to be my wife?"

"So she should just bow down to you and say how lucky she is? Come back down to reality, Log. You know better than anyone that sometimes you have to fight to get what you want."

My mom has a point. I got out of the neighborhood by putting every ounce of myself into my fighting. I got to be on the leaderboard of the MMA by continuing on that stride. And I remain on top because I never accept no. So why now, when that same gut feeling is tugging at me, the one I've never ignored before, am I not fighting to win her over?

I stare at the ring I'm twirling around my finger.

"Oh... I think you're thinking about booking the flight to Alaska," she singsongs.

"Thinking about it." I have ninety days before my next fight. Maybe in that time frame, I should see exactly what I can do to make sure that Nikki Greene stays Nikki Stone.

"I'll catch a flight and be up right after you."

I knew she wanted to go with me. She can be protective.

"Just give me at least a couple days on my own."

If there's one thing I figured out about Nikki last night, it's that she's not going to be running back into my arms— she might just knee me in the nuts.

"Why? Are you embarrassed by me?"

"I'll call you when things quiet down." I dodge the question. I'm not embarrassed of my mom, but I'm not sure how she'll fit in up in Alaska either.

"I'm proud of you, son. You're doing the right thing. Following your heart."

Once she puts it like that, I want to stomp my foot down on the brakes. Following your heart usually leads to heartbreak. And I don't want that.

"Thanks, Mom."

"Call me as soon as I can come up and meet her."

"I will. I'm not sure when that will be." I'll let Mom think it'll only be a little while. She has a hard time staying in the back seat when I'm driving my own life sometimes, but she means well always.

"I love you."

"And I love you. Be safe."

I hang up and twirl the silver wedding band around my finger. My mom is right that I have to go after her, if only to find out why I married her in the first place.

Chapter Five

Nikki

Since Molly and I returned to Sunset Bay this afternoon, I've been holed up in my house. All my siblings are at Truth or Dare Brewery since it's the night before tourist season kicks off. Everyone in town uses the excuse to party before our small town gets inundated with tourists. I have to make an appearance, but the fact that my mom has already called me twice and left voice messages to call her as soon as possible tells me she knows. It couldn't be a worse time for this news to come out since the entire family will be together tonight.

My phone dings again with a text from Molly.

Marla's on the hunt.

I blow out a breath and stare at myself in the mirror. I've done my hair, my makeup, and I don't look any different than when we left for our girls' trip. But I am different. I'm someone's wife.

Coming.

The Greene bunch are all here and accounted for. Fair warning.

Anyone saying anything?

Nope, but Adam keeps asking me questions about our trip.

Adam doesn't do gossip, so I'm sure he has no idea. Probably just making conversation so everyone doesn't hound him and Lucy about their honeymoon. They just returned as well.

Leaving in a few.

I put my purse crossways over my body and step outside of the house I rent with my sisters and stepsister. It's across the street from where my mom and stepdad live—the big house on the hill that was passed down to them by Ethel Greene, my step-grandma. I say step, but she's more my grandma than my own Greene grandma down in Arizona.

Our house is also right outside the downtown area of our small town, so I'm able to walk everywhere, even to work at the radio station. I don't want to think about returning there tomorrow morning and possibly facing the news about my impromptu wedding.

Couldn't I have at least married someone who wasn't famous? If I had, I could've slid it under the rug and no one would've known a thing. A quickie annulment later and I'd have moved on with my life. Something tells me this mess I'm in won't make it that easy.

I pass groups of people congregating in the different shops and along the shore of the bay. Everyone waves and says hello. No one says congratulations. That's a good sign that the news hasn't reached this far north yet.

Ten minutes later, my stomach is in knots as I open the door of my brothers' brewery, Truth or Dare. My big family sits around a large table to the left of the bar, and I say my hellos to people as I wind through the crowd.

Molly's already got a beer for me when I sit down across from her. I lean over and whisper, "Do you think she knows?"

Molly glances at where my mom is with the rest of my family. "She hasn't said anything, but she definitely wants to talk to you."

I sit back down on the stool.

"Nikki." Mom stands, waving at me.

As Mom tries to make her way over to me, a group of people step in front of her. Molly bites her lip, trying to hold back her laughter. I have to think of something and quick.

My brother, Jed, steps up next to Molly behind the bar and hands Molly a stack of empty glasses. "Holy shit, you're never going to believe who just walked in."

"Oh God, do I even want to know?" Clara, my step-brother Xavier's best friend, asks. "Someone from high school?"

"No." Jed glances back at the door.

Before I even try to look behind me, my stepbrother Cade interrupts. "Nikki, we pay Molly to work. You realize that, right?"

"Nikki!" My mom frantically waves. Thank goodness for the grandma in the walker Mom can't get around. "We need to talk."

"Logan Stone," Jed says and my eyes bulge at the same time my stomach sinks.

"Who's Logan Stone?" my sister Posey asks.

"The MMA fighter?" Xavier says.

"No shit!" Cameron, my stepbrother Fisher's best friend, turns toward the door as panic seizes my body. "Why would he be in Sunrise Bay?"

Chevelle says, "Oh, he's a hottie."

That earns her a glare from Cam.

"You know what, Cade, just leave me be. She's still working, and I need her advice. That's what bartenders do, right?" I snipe at Cade as though I can ignore the fact that my biggest mistake is about to be revealed in the middle of town for all to witness and gloat.

"Hey, Nik," Molly says, her eyes growing wide as she looks over my shoulder.

I put up my hand at my friend. Does she think I can't hear what's going on? I'm just in denial.

"You just had a girls' weekend. Why do you need to talk to her so bad?" Cade asks. "Not everything is urgent."

"Nik," Molly says again.

I swear I feel him behind me, as if we're two magnets and his energy pulls at me.

"Nik," Molly says louder this time.

"What?" I ask, and Molly points behind me.

I'm not an idiot. I know who's there, but when I turn around, it will become reality. I circle around in the stool to find Logan Stone in a pair of jeans, a T-shirt, and a sweatshirt. He's similar to how I left him, but he's clean-shaven now and his hair is styled. He looks good. Too good.

Jed finally lifts his jaw off the floor. "Hey, man, can I help you with something?"

Logan shakes his head, his eyes remaining locked with mine.

"Who is this guy?" Mandi nudges me with her elbow, and it's then I realize she'd approached me.

"I'm her husband," Logan says.

The entire restaurant quiets.

He cannot be serious. He had to announce that right here?

"Not really," I say, looking at all the stunned expressions on my family's faces.

"Nik," my mom says, catching her breath as if she ran a marathon to reach me. "We need to talk."

I glance at her and back at Logan. "In a minute, Mom."

I rise from the stool, grab Logan's hand, and tug him out of the brewery.

Let's just get this over with.

LOGAN ALLOWS me to pull him out to the sidewalk where I confront him. "What are you doing here?"

"You ran out on me," he says.

"Um... we were drunk. Surely you don't want to be married to me now that you've had some time to think about it."

He steps toward me. "I thought I was clear this morning that I wanted to talk."

I inhale a deep breath and cross my arms. "And I don't. It was a mistake."

He looks to his right and raises his eyebrows. I follow his gaze to see my family staring at us through the window. I tug him farther down the sidewalk so we're standing in front of Presley's bookstore.

"I don't think it was a mistake," he says like the crazy man he clearly is.

I throw up my hands. "You don't even know me."

He smiles and my stomach stirs with butterflies. It's a

knowing smile. That has to be how he won me over and got me to agree to marry him. "I want to get to know you."

I stare blankly at him and he laughs. Why does he seem to think everything is so funny?

"Okay, I'll admit, we had a good time on the balcony, but marriage? It was a decision fueled by alcohol."

"True." He shrugs as if that's neither here nor there.

"And how did you find me?"

A few people walk by and I hear whispers of my name. It's only a matter of time now.

"You had to fill your address out on the marriage license."

I groan. Of course—how did I not think about that?

"If you hadn't run out, I would have given it to you as a souvenir." He winks.

I narrow my eyes. "This isn't funny."

He holds up his hands. "I never said it was."

"I'm sure you could've found my phone number somehow. You didn't have to come to my hometown."

"And you would have answered my phone call?" he asks with one eyebrow quirking up.

He's right. I never would have answered.

I hear my name called from across the way, and I close my eyes. What did I do in my previous life to deserve this?

"You have no idea what you signed yourself up for," I murmur to him. I turn to my step-grandma, hugging her, "Ethel!" I nod in hello to her best friend. "Dori."

"Oh, you're new to town," Ethel says to Logan.

He holds out his hand. "Logan Stone, ma'am."

Ethel shoos him with her hand. "No ma'am. Makes me feel old." After she shakes his hand, her head volleys between the two of us. "How do you two know one another?"

"We're just friends," I lie, my eyes pleading with Logan to go along with me.

"Friends?" Dori says. "That's not what we heard." She puts out her hand toward Logan. "Big fan."

I should've known. They probably get together at the Northern Lights Retirement Center and chip in for pay-per-view or something.

"Thank you," Logan says and shakes her hand.

"Can I snap a picture? My grandsons are going to go crazy when I show them." Dori hands me her cell phone. "Get in, Ethel."

As I'm positioning Dori's phone to take the picture, Ethel looks at Logan. "I'm your grandma, by the way."

He smiles at her. "Lucky me."

They all turn to me and I snap the picture before handing the phone back to Dori. But the picture taking has grabbed a few Sunrise Bayers' attention and the whispering continues around us.

"Come on, let's go celebrate," Dori says, sliding her arm through Logan's and turning him back toward the brewery.

"Logan and I aren't done talking," I say to their retreating backs.

Ethel puts her arm around me. "Relax. Have some fun. Though last I heard, you might've had a little too much fun recently." She looks ahead of us. "Great ass."

"Ethel!" I screech.

She laughs. "Don't make me crush a Xanax in your drink to get you to loosen up."

"Nice. You're talking about drugging me? How grandmotherly of you."

"Technically, I'm your step-grandma, so I'm more fun." She winks.

We walk into the brewery, where Dori has Logan at my

family table already. He glances over his shoulder, and Molly comes up next to me once Ethel makes her rounds of hellos.

"So?" Molly asks.

"I don't know why he's here. We didn't get that far before we were accosted by Thelma and Louise there." I motion toward the two grandmas commanding most of the attention at the table.

"Oh, everyone knows why he's here. He's here for you."

I look at my best friend. "There's no way."

"Why not? Admit it, Nik, a hot MMA fighter tracked you down because he wants to give it a go with you. It's romantic if you ask me."

Jed comes up next to us. "Congratulations, sis. At least you picked a good one."

I scoff. "News sure travels fast."

"Welcome to Karmaville," Cade murmurs as he passes by with a plate of quesadillas for one of the tables.

I want to scream and punch and pout like a toddler, but I catch Logan's sparkling blue eyes on me, and what Molly said sinks in. He came all this way for me. For me. I can't say it doesn't feel good, but I don't know anything about my husband.

"Go over there and save the poor guy," Jed says, nudging me.

I slowly walk across the room. Logan's gaze never leaves mine while he dodges questions from my family.

"Tell us about the wedding," Posey says, and I'd like to kick her in the shin as I sink into a chair next to Logan.

Logan swings his arm around the back of my chair. "Nikki was a beautiful bride."

I shake my head. "No need to bullshit them." I roll my

eyes. "It was a Vegas wedding. We were drunk and neither of us remembers it. There, you all know now."

Adam outright laughs and Lucy elbows him in the ribs, so he feigns injury. Some of my family looks shocked, though most of the guys are still so enamored over the fact that Logan is sitting at the table with them, I'm not sure they even heard what I said.

"So tell me about my wife." Logan leans forward, resting his forearms on the edge of the table while Jed brings him a beer.

I slide my finger across my neck to tell my family to shut up and give them the death glare. But none of them can wait for the other to go first, so they all start talking at once. Aren't big families grand?

Chapter Six

Logan

"Logan should probably be going now," Nikki says, pinching my thigh under the table.

"Nah, I'm good."

She eyes me impatiently. "You must be tired."

I shrug. "Slept on the plane."

She groans.

"Do you have a private plane?" her brother or step-brother, I've yet to keep them all straight, asks. I need a cheat sheet if I don't want to embarrass myself.

"I don't own my own, but I did fly on a private jet."

"Must've been nice. When we flew back, this guy brought a six-course meal on the plane with him. He sat across the aisle from us, and the main course was fish." The bartender drops a few pitchers on the tables. "Can I get you something?" She sticks her hand out in front of me. "You probably don't remember me, but—"

"Molly, right?"

Her eyebrows shoot up in surprise.

I point at her name tag. "It's on your name tag."

Molly laughs and so does the rest of the table, which only seems to displease Nikki even more.

"Give me your most popular beer," I tell Molly.

"How about a Lucy Takes Flight? That way you can sample a bunch?" she says.

"That'd be great." I glance at Nikki, who's slouched in her chair with her head buried in her phone. "I don't usually drink beer, but I have three months before my next fight."

Nikki nods, disinterested. I might be in over my head here with her. Is it really worth fighting for her if she wants nothing to do with me?

"So, Logan," her mom, Marla, pipes up. "Can you give us any insight on the marriage thing since Nikki's decided to leave everyone in the dark?"

Nikki sits up straight. "Mom!"

"Well, you won't tell us anything and I want the details of my daughter's wedding."

"I told you we don't remember. We were drunk and the marriage will soon be annulled."

"Is that why you're here, Logan?" Marla asks me.

Nikki puts up her hand. "You don't have to worry about his answer because I'm answering for us."

"Actually, Mrs. Greene," I say, "I'm here to try to convince Nikki not to annul the marriage."

A smile creases Marla's lips. "Please call me Marla and do tell me more." She rests her chin in her palm.

"Okay, enough of this. This is our business, not any of yours." Nikki stands and glares at me. "Let's go talk then."

Finally! It's the reason I came here. Although her family seems great, I'd rather the two of us be on the same page in regard to this marriage sooner than later.

I stand, and Nikki stomps around me.

"This is the part where you follow her," the sister with red hair says. "And if you need a place to stay, come by the SunBay Inn. I own it."

I hadn't really thought about where I would stay for the time being, so I nod in appreciation. "Thanks. Good to meet you all."

Outside, Nikki allows me to walk alongside her, and we end up by the bay I have to assume this place is named after. A few people are around, but for the most part, we're secluded and no one can overhear us. She walks to the water's edge and picks up a few rocks.

"You can stop the Romeo act now," she mutters.

"Romeo act?"

"You just pranced in here on your white horse, ready to save me."

"I think those are two different love stories," I say, earning a glare that could make a serial killer run for his life. "I'm just saying."

"Listen..." She releases a breath and holds up her hand. "I appreciate you wanting to continue this, or even see what this could be. It's a real stand-up move." I open my mouth, but she doesn't allow me to speak before continuing. "But I could never be with someone like you."

Okay, that isn't what I thought she would say.

I narrow my eyes. "What do you mean?"

She tosses a rock into the water. "If we stay married and pursue this, what exactly do you think that would look like? You live in Vegas, and I live here."

"I don't live in Vegas."

She turns to me. "You don't?"

"No, I have a few houses, but none of them are in Vegas. Hence the suite in the casino."

She nods. "So where will you go after here?"

"You assume I'm leaving?" I smile, but it doesn't seem to improve her mood. I pick up my own rock and throw it into the water. "Probably Florida. That's where my mom is."

"Then you expect me to move to Florida? There's no MMA fighting stuff around here."

I look back at the small town. It's so different from anything I've ever experienced, but I like that there's no press up here. And although on the way here I didn't think much about how our distance would work, an idea sprouts in my head.

"I can train here for my fight."

"What?" Her head whips around. She clearly didn't expect that, and the fact that I surprised her makes my stomach stir with excitement.

"I have a fight in ninety days, like I said, and there's no reason I can't do that here. It's not that complicated. I'm sure I could find a space to put some gym equipment and everything else I need. That way you and I can get to know one another better and see if this is something we want to pursue."

"I already told you it isn't something I want to pursue." She chucks a rock into the water.

The entire trip up here, I contemplated how I would get her to agree to give me some time. Only one thing popped into my head. I don't want to bribe her to stay my wife, but if it buys me enough time to see if this could really be something between us, then maybe it's worth trying.

"What if we made a deal?"

She eyes me.

"You want to get that podcast up and running, right?"

Her face flushes pink and I'm guessing she forgot about

telling me that. "What about it?" Her posture is still defensive, but I can tell she's intrigued.

"I'll gladly do it, and I can get you a few other guests too."

"In exchange for what?" She crosses her arms over her ample chest.

Suddenly a memory of what it felt like to squeeze said chest in my hand surfaces and I have to shift my position to make room for the chub in my pants. "In exchange for giving this a chance while I train for my next fight."

"This seems like you're buying me off." She walks away from the water's edge and along the path that circles the bay.

I jog to catch up and fall in line with her. "I'm not buying you. I'm making a deal. You want to forget we ever got married and I want to see where this could go."

She stops and stares at me. "Give me one reason why you want to see where this goes. You know nothing about me. You were drunk when we got married too."

I shrug. "I'm letting my gut lead me here."

She laughs condescendingly. "Your gut? Your gut made you fly thousands of miles to a small town in Alaska, chasing some girl you haven't even known for twenty-four hours?"

"I also don't want the press on my back. They already reported that we got married. If it comes out that we've filed for an annulment or divorce, I'll have them hounding my every move and I need to prepare for the fight."

"So you want to pretend, you mean?" Her tone isn't one of complete distaste anymore.

I figure although it's not the complete truth, I might as well just go with it now if it gets her to agree. "Yeah."

It is part of the truth. I can't focus when the press is all over me. If I hide up here and we do an interview that says we're happily married, then they'll grow disinterested when there's no juicy gossip.

She's quiet while she practically speed walks around the bend. "And you'd arrange for some other big names to do my podcast?"

"Yep, and I have a connection to a satellite radio guy."

She sighs and stops, heading over to a hill and sitting. "You're making it hard to pass up."

"That was my intention." I sit down next to her, propping my knees up.

She looks at me. "Only you and I would know about our deal?"

"I can see that you're close to your family. But the more people who know, the higher the chance that it gets out. I've seen the press do some pretty shady things to get people to talk, so I think it would be better if you and I were the only ones who know about our arrangement. It's better if everyone thinks we're a happy couple."

"True. I hate deceiving my family though." She lowers her head between her knees.

And I hate deceiving her. But clearly the whole "wearing my heart on my sleeve" thing isn't going to work with her. She doesn't believe in gut feelings and intuition. Hopefully I'll find out why someday because she'll trust me enough to tell me. Until then, I'll just keep crossing my fingers behind my back.

"But you'll finally get that podcast up and running."

She tilts her head and rests her cheek on her knees. I want to tuck a strand of her blond hair behind her ear, but she'd probably find it creepy.

"Okay," she says in a soft tone. "But it stays between us."

"Between us," I say.

"And you're going to stay up here and train?"

"Yeah, but first things first, you have to do one interview in Vegas with me to get the press off our backs."

She nods. "Okay."

We don't shake hands or seal it with a kiss, but the deal is made. I have three months to prove to her that there's a reason we got married in Vegas. Wish me luck. I'll need all of it I can get.

Chapter Seven

Nikki

I'm delusional. That's got to be the reason I've agreed to continue this sham of a marriage with Logan.

When I walk into the radio station office, the administrative staff all peer up at me from their computers. A few say hello, but I beeline into the recording studio to get my segment over with. I have to tell my listeners about my marriage so that they'll continue to trust me. After this, I'm flying down to Vegas with Logan to do an interview where we'll say we're happily married. Such an interview is necessary according to Logan.

"Hey, Chip," I say, sliding into my seat in front of the microphone.

"I have a whole list of questions that won't stop coming in about you and a certain MMA fighter?" my older co-host says with a laugh.

Chip used to run the segment I do now, but he's happy

co-hosting with me—probably because I take the brunt of the feedback when Sunrise Bayers are upset at something we've reported.

"And I'll answer them."

"What about him? Is he coming in?" The only reason Chip is asking is because I'm sure he wants an autograph.

"No. I'm handling this on my own."

I ignore his pout while he stands to refill his coffee mug. My gut has been clenching so hard, I've yet to finish my morning smoothie.

Chip returns a minute later, and our producer, Matty, tells us we're on air in two minutes. I gear up, hoping to satisfy the town with my openness about the situation, even though I'm lying through my teeth.

Matty counts us down behind the window and points at us.

I reposition my headphones and straighten in my chair. "Hello, Sunrise Bayers! It's Nikki Greene and I'm here with Chip."

Chip says hello in his faux grumpy voice.

"Let's cut to the chase, shall we?" I say, my stomach churning. "I think when MMA fighter Logan Stone came to town, everyone was on the edge of their seats. I know for a fact my brothers were drooling over the man."

"So were your sisters," Chip adds.

I laugh and shake my head. "Rumors are flying, and here at 'Scandals of Sunrise Bay,' I like to report the truth, as you all know. The truth is that I married Logan Stone in Las Vegas this past weekend."

Chip presses a button and wedding bells ring.

"Thank you, Chip. It was unexpected and a hasty decision, but we've decided to see where it goes." I can't believe I've lied to my listeners for the first time ever.

"Did you know him before?" Chip asks. I give him a scathing look and he holds up a question card. "One of our listeners wants to know."

Truth, Nikki. Tell as much as you can.

"No. As most of you know, my best friend, Molly, is a fanatic about MMA fighting, so when we booked our girls' weekend away, she bought front row tickets to the fight. One thing led to another, and by morning, I was married. That's the truth, Sunrise Bayers, and that's about all I'm willing to let you in on right now."

Chip holds up a stack of paper. "We have a few more questions."

"Are they asking about my marriage?"

"Someone wants to know if you're registered somewhere?"

I laugh. "Oh, we're perfectly fine. Please do not buy us anything."

"Another one wants to know where you're going to live?" Chip keeps asking questions even with me slicing my finger along my throat.

"What do you mean?"

He raises his hands. Then it dawns on me that I have no idea where we're going to live. Surely Logan doesn't think we're going to live together.

Matty sends in a call and Chip answers it. Damn him.

"Looks like I get to spread the word for once here," Chip says. "We have a caller who just reported that Logan Stone has signed a lease for the old Linville house on the bay."

I'm silent because the old Linville house is gorgeous. It needs some rehab, but the wraparound porch that looks out over the bay is its best feature. It's usually rented out for tourist season well in advance, so I have no idea how Logan swindled the deal.

"My guess is you're moving into the Linville house now, Nikki. Movin' on up," Chip says with a laugh.

I'd like Chip to go back to his grumpy self who doesn't add a ton to my segment.

"Details to be reported another time. In other news…" I begin the next segment because I'm over talking about myself at this point.

When Chip and I end our segment, I catch sight of Logan in the booth with Matty. What the hell?

"And that's all for today, Sunrise Bayers. See you tomorrow." I click the "off the air" button before Matty allows Logan to come in.

"Great job, guys, and your man is here to see you, Nik," Matty says through the booth.

"I'll be right out."

I hang up my headphones and grab my stuff. Chip is so close behind me on the way out, I can barely get through the door without feeling his breath on my neck.

"Chip," I say, glaring behind me.

He has a piece of paper and pen in his hand. "I want an autograph."

By the time I reach the hallway, Logan's walking out of the production booth with Matty as though they're old friends, talking about the fight from the other night and how Logan doesn't look that beat up. The bruises on his jaw are already healing. I definitely need to ask him why he does what he does at some point.

"Hey," I say.

Logan shoves his hands into his pockets and gives me the cutest shy look ever, as though he's embarrassed or something. A girl could get addicted to a look like that coming from such an intimidating figure.

"Hi. Hope you don't mind," he says, his voice lower than when he was talking to Matty.

"It's fine. We have to go anyway, right?"

He nods.

Chip clears his throat behind me, and I step aside. "Do you mind signing something for Chip?"

Logan's hands spring out of his pockets and he accepts the pen and paper from Chip. He signs his name then hands it back.

"Thanks," Chip says, staring at the piece of paper as though he's a six-year-old boy who just met his idol.

Logan smiles at him. "No problem."

We all stand in the awkwardness for a moment before I break the silence. "Okay, well, we have to get going."

Logan shakes Matty's hand then Chip's. "It was great meeting you both."

"Stop by anytime," Matty says and runs his hand through his sandy-blond hair.

"Yeah," Chip adds, still looking a little starstruck.

Oh boy, we need to get out of here.

I lead us out of the radio station to find a black SUV waiting at the curb.

"The plane is ready for us," Logan says.

I nod and slide in as though I'm used to this kind of treatment, ignoring the people's stares.

AN HOUR LATER, we're in the air. Being on a private plane is surreal. The flight attendant isn't some young thing with her skirt right below her ass though. She doesn't bend down to show Logan her cleavage, and it's nice to see her wedding ring when she hands me a sparkling water with lemon.

Logan stares out at the mountains below us. "Alaska really is a beautiful state."

"Yep." I take a sip of my water.

"Have you lived here all your life?" He turns to me, and the blue of his eyes strikes me again.

If I trusted my instincts when it came to men, his eyes would say he's trustworthy and kind. But I don't.

"I grew up in Arizona. After my parents divorced, my mom moved us to Sunrise Bay since my grandparents still lived there. She grew up there. She rekindled her relationship with Hank and ended up marrying him. He's my dad's cousin."

I figure why hide it? Someone will dig up that juicy piece of information and Logan shouldn't be caught by surprise like he is now. Actually, he looks as if he's trying to decipher whether I'm telling the truth or not.

I touch his arm. Damn, it's hard. "Yeah, my dad and Hank are cousins, so my mom never had to change her name." I give him a saccharine smile.

"So your stepbrothers and sister?"

I nod. "Yeah, they're also blood related to me. I think it's like third cousins or something." I wave it off. "But we're just one twisted, happy family."

I hate that it comes off that way. I love Hank like a dad. In many ways, he's been more of a dad than my own all these years.

"That's interesting."

I laugh. "Yeah, that's a word for it." I sip my drink. "So where are you from if you don't live in Las Vegas?"

"Florida. Well, my mom lives there now, but I grew up in Indiana. We never go back there though. Once I got my first check, I moved us both to Florida. She lives there full time and I go see her as often as I can."

Great. He's a momma's boy. "That's nice."

"So I was used to the cold when I was younger, but not so much anymore."

"Good thing our three months together are during our spring to summer season then."

He laughs. "True. So you think you're a Sunrise Bay lifer?"

"Yeah. As much as I complain about my family, I can't imagine not living near them. Like I said, we're twisted."

"I'm kind of jealous. When I grew up, it was just me and my mom."

I have a feeling I could ask him any question I wanted and he'd be honest with me.

"Big families are great, don't get me wrong, but take this for example." I wave my finger between us. "They're in our business the entire time. Even now, I'm getting texts about you renting the Linville house."

"Well, I had to have somewhere to live, and my team needs a place to stay, so the guest quarters are what sold me."

I turn to face him and cross my legs. His eyes dip to follow the movement and my stomach swirls with butter-flies. I can see why my drunken side married him.

"How did you score it? I mean, tourist season started today and I'm sure they had it rented out."

He shrugs.

"Tell me."

"I offered them a lot of money."

"And the poor people who had their vacation planned already?"

"I'm putting them up at Glacier Point Resort in Lake Starlight. I heard it's nice."

I huff. Glacier Point Resort is the fancy hotel in our

parts. I'm surprised he's not just staying there. "That's nice of you."

"I wasn't going to ruin someone's vacation. Luckily they all agreed." His finger runs along the stitching of the seat. "It's weird for me sometimes."

"What is?"

"Growing up, I was dirt poor. My mom worked three jobs and I never had new clothes until I got my own job. To be able to rent that place and move my entire staff up to Sunrise Bay for three months?" He shakes his head. "Sometimes I think it's a dream."

There he goes again with this vulnerable side that tugs at my heart. I haven't done a ton of research on Logan because I haven't had time. Which is probably a good thing. I'd be disappointed to find out that the Logan I'm getting isn't the real one.

"It isn't." I look around the private plane. "Amazing what just using your fists can get you."

He tilts his head. "You think I'm just a dumb guy who makes millions by fighting people?"

I shake my head. "I'm not sure what I think at this point."

And that's the truth. I'll never lie to someone to make them feel better, but so far, I still wonder what really happened on that balcony for me to agree to marry him.

"One last thing," he says and digs into his pocket.

"What?"

"You should probably wear this." He holds out the diamond ring I left in the hotel room. It looks so expensive, I'm scared to be responsible for it.

I glance at the flight attendant situated in the back, reading a magazine.

"I'll return it after this is over." I slide it on my left ring finger. The ring is stunning. Drunk me certainly knows what I like and isn't afraid to ask for it.

"No rush." He straightens up and drinks his water.

I hope I have the strength to get through this without falling for this man, because I get the distinct feeling he could break my heart if I let him.

Logan

We're in a black SUV on the way to the interview Vince set up. I agreed that we'd talk to one person and the news can spread from there. I picked the man I trust the most, Rick Dean. He's always been truthful when it comes to me, and I trust he won't try to dig up anything I don't tell him.

"Have you been to Vegas before?" I stupidly ask Nikki as she stares out the window.

She smiles at me with an expression that says, "Think about what you just asked."

"I mean other than your trip with Molly."

She shakes her head. "No, and we didn't really get to do that much either."

"Well, if you want, we could stay the night and see some sights. I can get us into a show."

"Me, you, and this town only seem to cause trouble. Maybe we should fly out right away." She's been smiling more since we got on the plane. It's a welcome change from all the scowls I got yesterday.

"Vegas has a lot to offer. I'd love to show you around." I find myself searching for excuses as to why we could spend a little more alone time here.

"Let's play it by ear. One thing I know I don't want to do is gamble."

I laugh because other than when I first arrived in town all those years ago, you'd never find me at the tables. "Deal."

The SUV pulls along the curb of the casino where Vince booked a room to conduct the interview. Of course, Vince is waiting outside, pacing.

I lean across her and point at him. "That's Vince."

"He looks intense. He's your manager?" She turns to ask me, and our faces end up mere inches from one another's.

What I wouldn't do to kiss her again.

"Yeah, and intense is a good way to describe him."

The driver opens the door and Vince rushes over. "Thank God, what on Earth took so long? Rick is already here."

Nikki steps out, then I do, but I grab her hand and pull her into the casino before anyone on the street can spot us. Vince walks us right to the elevators and we slide in as someone points and says my name.

I like it a lot better when we use back entrances. The fact that Vince didn't arrange one says he wants people to get a glimpse of my new bride. He's always using some leverage to get me in the media

"Nikki, this is Vince. Vince, this is Nikki."

She takes her hand out of mine to shake Vince's hand and I catch him looking her up and down. Nikki slides closer to me as though she's creeped out.

"Nice to meet the woman who pinned down Logan," he says with distaste in his voice.

"Cool it, Vince," I say.

Now Nikki's shoulder is pressed to mine. I entwine our fingers to put her at ease. To my delight, she doesn't pull away. I guess we have the excuse of making Vince believe this thing between us is real, but I still feel good that her automatic response wasn't repulsion.

The elevator doors open, and we follow Vince down the hallway to the room. Rick is inside, along with his camera crew. Looks as though someone arranged for a fruit tray, small sandwiches, and some drinks.

Rick stands and heads our way. "Log! How the hell are you?" He gives me a handshake and turns his attention to Nikki. "Aren't you the lucky one?"

Nikki narrows her eyes slightly. "Don't you think he's the lucky one?"

Rick pretends not to be embarrassed, but the tips of his ears turn pink. "Yes, of course. I mean, you're both lucky to have found love in this city where people usually end up down on their luck."

He's tall and thin and usually smokes like a chimney, but never in front of me. I told him at the first interview that if he lit up, I'd knock him out. I don't want that shit near my lungs.

"Let's get started. I want to be one of the first to wish you well on your marriage." Rick sits down, signaling to his camera guy.

"Thank you." I put my hand on the small of Nikki's back, leading her to the couch. "Let's keep away from topics like where we'll be living and where Nikki is from. I don't want anyone harassing us there."

Rick nods as he looks at his papers but glances up. "You do know people will find out anyway."

"Let them dig it up on their own. I'm not giving up the information willingly."

Nikki sends me an appreciative smile.

"All right then. We have some pictures Vince gave us. Can we show those?" Rick asks.

Nikki groans, but doesn't say anything.

"We'd prefer you didn't. We'll be upfront that we weren't exactly stone-cold sober when we wed, but I don't think people need to see those pictures."

"You're killing me right now, Logan." Rick sighs.

"If you don't want the interview, I'll find someone else." I go to stand, and he holds up his hand.

"No. Sit down. I'll make do. Just come off like you just got out of bed fucking for the last day."

Nikki fidgets in her seat, and I wrap my arm around her, resting my palm on her shoulder.

I lean in and whisper, "Just relax. I'll do most of the talking."

She nods, and I kiss her temple. She tries to veer away, but I hold her firm against me and she finally realizes why. All eyes are on us.

"Let's get this rolling." Rick signals toward the camera.

Nikki straightens her back, placing her palm on my thigh as though it's as natural as crossing her legs. My dick stirs in my pants, but there's no time to address it since the cameras are rolling, so I put on a smile and hope like hell I'm as good an actor as I am a fighter.

AN HOUR AND A HALF LATER, we're out of the hotel room, saying goodbye to Rick.

"Back to the airport?" Nikki asks.

Vince is lingering. I wish he'd go away at this point, but he's adamant about talking to me without Nikki.

"I thought we could at least catch a show and dinner," I say.

Nikki purses her lips. She does that a lot, I've noticed, but not in a mean way. She does it when she's thinking. Almost like she weighs the good and the bad of every decision. "But we can go home first thing in the morning?"

I nod. "Yes."

"You two should definitely go out and be seen together. Let people snap pictures and ask for autographs." Vince butts in.

Nikki looks at him and back at me. I'm not sure she cares for Vince very much. "What am I going to wear?"

I grab her hand, linking our fingers. "Did you know Vegas has great shopping?" I tug her down the hallway. "I'll catch you later, Vince."

"Log!" he calls.

"I said later."

We step into the elevator and the doors close on a very unhappy Vince. But there's no way I can handle him telling me how to handle this right now. Being with Nikki is the first time I've felt like myself in so long. Before I was Logan Stone, MMA fighter.

"You can talk to him. I'm sure I can keep myself busy." Nikki loosens her hand out of my grip.

I let her, but as soon as the elevator doors open, I'll be grabbing it again. Especially if we're spotted. "No. I want to spend the day with you. You're nice enough to do all this for me. I want to pay you back with a nice meal and show."

"You're paying me back by getting me five guests for my podcast," she says in a tone that suggests I might've forgotten my end of the deal.

"I know. Don't worry. I'll get them for you."

The elevator doors open, and I take her hand. It's so petite and soft. I love the way it feels in mine.

We're on the casino floor in no time, and I walk us out the doors and into a waiting cab at the cab stand. It doesn't take long to reach some stores attached to one of the expensive hotels. Nikki is skeptical about picking anything, so I hand the salesperson a few dresses for Nikki to try on.

While she's doing that, I dial up Vince just to make sure he stays off my back tonight.

"You can't just blow me off like that," Vince answers without a hello.

"I don't wanna talk about what angle you want to use this marriage for. I'm calling because I'll be staying up in Sunrise Bay for the three months before the fight. I've sent messages and talked to all the trainers. Everyone will be joining me up there."

"You can't be serious! You have the gym here and in Florida. Why not just go to your mom's if you want a change?" There's anger in his voice that he's trying to control.

When I was starting out, Vince never got angry with me, but that's because I always did what he wanted. Now that I make a lot of my own decisions, he lets it be known when he doesn't agree.

"Nikki is my wife. That's where she's from, so that's where I'll be. I've already rented a house for both her and me and also for the trainers and chef." It's not easy to transport your entire regime thousands of miles, but spending my off time with Nikki is worth the expense. There's no way this would work if I was down here and she was up there. At least not for the end goal I'm hoping to achieve.

"She's your *Vegas* wife. I have no idea why you're so hell-bent on trying to make this thing work."

"What are you even talking about?" I whisper, seeing someone point me out to his wife. I lower my head.

"This charade of yours. I know you met her that night. That you only married her because you were drunk." I hear ice clinking into a cup. The fact Vince is drinking this early in the day says I've stressed him out more than I thought.

"Good thing I don't have to get permission from you to live my life. I'm being courteous by telling you what's going on. The training will happen up there. You can come up and visit if you'd like, but I won't be doing any more interviews."

"You're gonna tank your career. She's a distraction."

I look up to see Nikki in front of a three-way mirror. The saleswoman is zipping up the back of her black dress. It hugs her curves and shows off her great ass. Vince is right. She's a distraction, but the best kind of distraction.

"This is my decision. I'm not asking you to agree. I gotta go." I hang up and pocket my phone, walking back into the store.

I sit in one of the chairs by the mirror. Nikki catches me in the reflection, and now that I see the front of the dress, I want to hand my credit card to the saleswoman and tell her she'll wear it out of the store, but it's Nikki's decision, not mine.

"Do you like it?" Nikki asks while looking at me through the mirror.

"I could show you how much I like it, but we'd be arrested for public indecency."

The saleswoman giggles, and Nikki shakes her head at

my attempt at humor. This time I'm not rewarded with that smile of hers.

Okay, she doesn't care for crude jokes, got it.

"I'll take it then." Nikki steps down and heads back to the dressing room.

"Here's my card. She needs shoes and a shawl to cover up when we're around others."

"What?" Nikki says, stomping back over to me. She plucks the credit card out of the saleswoman's hands and holds it back out to me. "I do not need a shawl, and I'll be paying for it myself."

"I told you it was my treat." I take the card from between her fingers and hand it back to the saleswoman.

Nikki grabs it again. "I don't want to owe you anything."

"Fine. I'll buy her the shawl."

She stomps her foot. God, I love her feistiness. Makes me want to throw her over my shoulder and carry her off to bed. If only we were there already. "No."

"Yes." I look at the saleswoman. "If you could give us a moment." She walks away, and I set my gaze on Nikki. "Please let me do this. I want to do this."

She cocks her hip and stares at me. "I'll let you buy the dress, but no shawl. First of all, I'm not eighty."

"And second of all?"

She steps closer to me, and the scent of her perfume wafts up to my nostrils, making my dick strain in my pants. "I'm not someone who cheats. Other guys can look, but I'm all yours."

She turns around and heads to the dressing room, leaving me speechless. I want to follow her, lock the door, and press her against the wall.

Fuck, I'm in deeper than I thought.

Chapter Nine

Nikki

We're back in Logan's suite at the hotel so that no one will know we're spending the night in two different bedrooms. I put on the earrings that I had to practically put his hands in handcuffs so he wouldn't buy them and look at myself in the mirror. It feels as though it's been ages since I dressed up this nice.

When I walk out to the shared living space, Logan stands with a drink in his hand by the window. He turns toward me, and I smile at the man I hardly know but am married to.

"So?" I twirl around.

"Just like at the store, I'm speechless." He sets down his drink and walks over to me. His black suit forms to his body as if it was made specifically for him, and I'm sure it probably was. "Allow me." He must remember from the store that I can't zip up the dress on my own.

I turn around, and his fingers graze my spine until they

reach the zipper. The dress pulls snugger as he zips it up to where it stops mid-back.

"There you go." The hoarseness in his voice says he felt what I did, and a shiver runs up my spine.

"Thank you." I turn around to face him, and his gaze soaks me in once more, stirring my desire. "We should go."

"Yeah. Definitely." He grabs his wallet and phone from a tray by the couch and pockets them before meeting me by the door.

We walk down the hall to the elevator, and it comes in no time at all, as though those who have suites are serviced before the other thousands of guests.

After we step in, the space is quiet and awkward, so I decide to fill the silence. "Are you always in the same suite?"

He glances over from staring at the numbers as we descend. "No, but since my fight is here, the suite comes with the contract."

"Oh, that's nice."

"It is, because I usually train in Vegas when I'm this close to a fight."

The doors open, but we're underground. Another black SUV is waiting for us.

"You pulled out all the stops, huh?" I say.

"I don't want tonight ruined with me signing autographs and people asking me how I managed to beat Hector Garcia the other night. Everyone has their fans, and surprisingly, I'm not always theirs." He opens the door, waving off the driver, and I laugh while sliding in.

He follows. The back seat feels claustrophobic with us so close and dressed so nice, like this is a real date. To the outside world, it has to look like that, but now I'm struggling not to let it feel like it is.

This dress was way too expensive, and I should've never agreed to let him buy it.

"So how did you beat Hector Garcia?" I ask, not really knowing anything about what he does.

He looks at me from the corner of his eye in a suspicious manner. "I thought you didn't like fighting?"

"I don't."

He turns his big body my way. "Why?"

"I don't like blood." That's the best I can do to describe why I hate it so much. When Jed was younger and got into a fight, it made my stomach turn, but I can't put a specific reason on why.

"Fair enough." He straightens in his seat. "But if you want to know, I do a lot of research before a fight. I examine my opponent's strengths, his weaknesses, and watch films of his previous fights. My trainers help me a lot. In all honesty, when I'm in the ring, it's the adrenaline that helps me the most."

"Do you ever think about getting hurt?"

He chuckles. "At first, I did, but belief in myself pushes that fear away. Belief that I'm the better fighter and I'll come out the victor. If you worry about whether it's going to hurt, you pull your own punches, and that's not a path to victory."

I can't deny that this confident side of him who knows he's the best at what he does is attractive as hell. "Glad it's worked out well for you so far."

He nods but doesn't look over. "The next fight is the true test. Brett Rinaldo. He's younger than me and on the rise. People are saying he might be my demise."

Vulnerability laces his tone. I have no idea how he trusts me so much with only knowing me such a short time.

"I'm sure you'll win."

"I know I'll win." He winks, and that vulnerable side of him disappears, replaced with his arrogant one.

I'm reminded that I don't know this man. Not the true Logan Stone, at least. I'm doing him a favor, and in return, he's thanking me by taking me out on the town. This is a business arrangement and nothing more—even if we are legally married.

Thankfully, I don't have to make any more small talk because the SUV pulls up along the curb in front of a restaurant. The valet opens our door and Logan steps out first, holding out his hand for me to take. I step out, and we make our way inside but have to hop on an elevator first.

When we step out, the windows give a view of the Strip all lit up at night. The hostess escorts us to a secluded table by the window, and I'm so in awe of the view, I miss the fact that Logan is waiting for me to sit down so he can tuck in my chair.

"Oh, sorry." I sit and he pushes me into the table. "It's beautiful."

Logan folds himself into a chair across from me. "The first time I came to Vegas, a promotor took me here, and I thought to myself, 'I'm either going to leave here broke and embarrassed or my name will be lit up in lights.' It just feels like there's no in-between when it comes to this town, you know?"

This man changes personalities like I change outfits.

"And now you're on billboards." I point at a juice cleansing ad featuring his face across the street.

"Could've gone either way." He shrugs.

Our server comes over and Logan asks if he can order us a bottle of wine. I say yes, of course, because wine is rarely a bad idea, and she disappears to go make it happen.

"If you don't like it, feel free to get whatever you want," he says.

I pick up the menu and scan the array of steaks and side dishes. There are no prices, so I lower the menu and look at him. "We didn't have to go somewhere so…"

"It's the only place I could get reservations at," he says with a gleam in his eye that says that's not the case. "I'd be happy to order for you."

I tip the menu down again. "That's okay."

He looks a bit sheepish. "Actually, if we split a steak and fish dish, it would be better for my diet. I love their steaks and usually reserve this place when I'm done with a fight, but this time I'm headed right back into training."

I lower my menu. Usually, I wouldn't be cool with someone else ordering for me, but I intrigued. "Okay."

"Really?" His eyes widen.

"Yeah. As long as it's not juice."

He laughs and sets down his menu. "They're actually good. I have some back at the suite. We'll take it back to Sunrise Bay with us."

His sentence throws me for a moment. It's almost as though we're a real couple. As though we go everywhere together.

I glance around the room. "Speaking of…"

As I'm about to talk about the Linville house and the expectations of us pretending to be happily married, the server returns. She's flirty with Logan, but I suspect that's her normal personality. Plus, he's not really mine, so I can't be upset even if that's a sharp stab of jealousy in my chest. He orders us the steak and tilapia with a side of vegetables and every potato they make.

She leaves and I'm about to ask my question, but he beats me to it. "I wasn't sure what potato you prefer."

"I'm assuming those aren't on your diet?"

He shrugs. "I'm going to cheat a bit today." He lifts his glass. "To new beginnings."

I raise my glass and we clink them before each taking a sip.

"So, the Linville house?" I ask.

"Yeah, it really is amazing. The deck by the water—"

"I'm curious, if we're..." I look around, but we're pretty secluded. Still, I lean in and lower my voice. "If we're supposed to be a couple, won't we have to live together?"

"I assumed so. That's why I gave the trainers and chef the guest quarters in the back. You can stay with me in the main house. But you'd have your own bedroom if you'd like."

He really has thought about everything. Although it's slightly disappointing that I'm finally married and not reaping the rewards of regular sex with a man like him. "Perfect. I live with my sisters now, so we can move some of my stuff over when we get back."

He smiles and sips his wine again.

"Is there anything else we need to discuss?" I ask, trying to tick off all the boxes.

"How about we just enjoy the night? We can discuss any issues as they come up."

I don't usually work that way. I prefer to do lists. Not that I'm super organized or anything, but I don't like to leave balls in the air. Still, I can't think of anything else to go over at the moment, so I let him turn the conversation to Alaska and how his trainers are excited to take him on some hikes and try some new things that will push his training to a new level.

The food comes. Logan eats the majority of both meals,

but there's not a lot of room in my dress, so I'm okay with that.

After dinner, he takes me to a Cirque du Soleil show where the final act is a man and a woman working with an aerial strap. The audience watches with bated breath as they rise and fall over the stage, suspended in the air as they twirl flawlessly.

All I can think of is how much that woman trusts that man to make sure she doesn't plummet to her death. I'm not sure I could ever accomplish that.

The curtains draw closed, and the lights flicker on.

Logan smiles at me in the mezzanine of our private viewing booth. "Did you enjoy it?"

"I did."

He reaches forward and his thumb brushes across my cheek. I must look puzzled because he raises his thumb. His skin is wet.

"Oh, sorry." I swipe the tears away before he can try to do it again. "Is my makeup messed up?"

He shakes his head. "You look beautiful."

Standing, he holds out his hand for me and I accept it. We walk out a back entrance and the SUV is already waiting there. The night feels almost magical, and I wish for a moment that our marriage was real. To relive this night over and over with him would be no hardship. But it's not, and if we were really married, he'd never stare at me like he just did—as though I was the most beautiful woman he's ever laid eyes on. At least not for long. All men eventually tire of a woman's beauty and go looking for the next one.

My feet are killing me as we walk up to the penthouse. As soon as we're inside, I slide off my heels and sit on the couch. Logan stands by the door for a second, his eyes on me.

"What?" I ask.

"Just..." He shakes his head.

"What?" I tuck my legs under my body on the couch.

"Either it's déjà vu or you did that after we got married."

Our gazes lock, and that pull I've felt all night between us grows stronger, as though someone is pulling the string between us from both ends. "Maybe you're used to having a lot of girls up here and that's where the mix-up is."

His smile falls. "I'm not the playboy you like to think I am." He slides off his own shoes and joins me on the couch. "I know we ate, but you hardly ate a thing. Want some room service?"

"Truffle fries?" I ask.

"Sold."

He picks up the phone and orders. I'm certain we didn't do this after we were married.

Chapter Ten

Logan

"Here." I bring out a pair of sweatpants and a T-shirt for Nikki. "They'll be too big, but see what you can do."

"The embarrassing thing will be if they aren't too big." She picks them up and disappears into her bedroom.

I check my emails on my phone for a minute and then Nikki walks out of her bedroom wearing my gray sweatpants that are rolled up at the bottom more than a few times. "They'll work."

She sits on the couch and I realize—this is what I want. Someone to share my time with. I'm usually surrounded by people. Vince, the trainers, cooks, other fighters, you name it. But I wouldn't mind someone being here because they *want* to be here, not because I'm paying them.

Then again, if I think hard about it, Nikki's only here because I swindled a deal with her.

The knock at the door means the food is here. Perfect timing.

I answer the door and two guys bring in two trays of food on carts. I ask if they'll put them on the coffee table in the living area, and I sign the bill and they leave.

Nikki leans forward and removes the lid off one of the plates. "Potato skins!"

"I knew you didn't eat enough at dinner." I sit and take the lids off all the platters. There isn't much nutrition in front of us, but I'll suffer the consequences tomorrow.

"That dress didn't leave me any room." She eats another bite while knocking a straw packaged in paper on the table to get it loose to put in her water.

I sit back and watch her enjoying herself, but she notices.

"Why aren't you eating?" She chokes down the rest of her bite and covers her mouth with a napkin.

"I am." I slide to the edge of the couch. "How about we get to know one another?"

She grabs a nacho and dips it in salsa. "What do you have in mind?"

"If we're gonna keep up the charade of our marriage, I need to know some important things."

That grabs her attention. "True." Sitting back on the couch, she brings the plate of nacho chips to her lap. "You go first."

"Favorite color?" I grab a carrot off the veggie platter.

"Seriously? I'm pigging out on nachos and potato skins and you're going to graze vegetables like a rabbit?" She reaches for another potato skin. "Good thing we're already married."

I laugh. "I'm still full from dinner. If you want more, let me know. I'll call room service again."

She sticks out her tongue at me then makes a show of biting into the potato skin.

"So, favorite color?"

"Black."

"Black?" I ask.

"Just kidding. Red."

"The color of love? I thought you didn't believe in love?" I take a sip from my water.

"Why do you say that?"

"Am I wrong?" I'm probably venturing into territory I shouldn't. Maybe I should've waited to ask her such a deep question, but in order for me to figure out how to win her over, I have to know what I'm up against. She's already made it pretty clear she's not a big believer in marriage.

"You're not wrong. I'm a product of divorce." She moves the plate back onto the table and grabs a water. I hope I didn't ruin her appetite.

"That's right. Kissing cousins."

She frowns, then shakes her head. "You have no idea how many times I've had to tell people that my mom and Hank are not cousins. Enough about me. What's your favorite color?"

"Black."

"Hardy har har. Really, what is it?"

"Green."

"The color of money? I'm surprised red isn't your favorite color."

I snap off a piece of celery. "Why's that?"

"It's the color of blood."

"Is that payback for my kissing cousins remark?"

She gives me a smirk. "No. I don't play games."

"I don't either."

"Next question?" She brings the platter of nachos back to her lap, which is a clear indication that talking about love or her parents' divorce isn't something she's comfortable with.

So I ask, "What's your favorite food? Nachos or potato skins?"

"Ha. Actually, Twinkies. What about you?"

"Ho Hos." She gives me a glare and I laugh. "What? Apparently we both like creamy fillings?" She throws a chip at me and I pick it up and eat it.

"Oh, so you are human. You *can* eat a nacho chip?"

"You're a bad influence."

"Please, what would you be doing if you weren't here with me? Probably out at some club, getting bottle service while girls hang all over you."

I like to think that there's jealousy in her tone, but maybe that's hopeful thinking. "I'd probably be in bed."

"With how many women?" She gives me a smug smile.

I narrow my gaze. "By myself."

"I highly doubt that."

"I'm kind of a boring guy outside of beating the shit outta guys for money."

"Tell me why you do it—other than for the money."

I grab the veggie platter and situate myself on the corner of the couch. "I didn't realize we were gonna get this deep. If I answer, then you'll have to answer what you have against love."

She's quiet for a moment and I think she might tap out, but she nods.

"I grew up in a shitty neighborhood and got picked on. Eventually I fought back, earned myself some respect, and I liked the feeling. Vince was from the same neighborhood and saw me sparring with a guy and wanted to work with me to bring me onto the circuit. I didn't have any other options and figured using my fists rather than my brains was an easier way to earn a living." She doesn't have to know the long road it took to get here and how scared I am that it's all coming to a close. Maybe not in the next ninety days, but eventually, I'll have to retire. "The money is good though."

"So you like the fact that people look up to you?"

I shake my head. "No. I like the fact that people don't treat me like a piece of shit."

Her lips tip down. I probably should've kept that to myself.

I raise my hand before she can chime in with some half-assed attempt to make me feel better. "I'm far from that scrawny kid who got cornered in the alley of our neighborhood every week, but winning makes me feel powerful and I've grown addicted to it." I shrug.

"What will happen when you don't win?" She switches the nachos for the potato skins.

"I think that time is growing closer. This fight against Brett Rinaldo in a few months... some people think it'll be my demise. That I'll have to give up the title and never come back from it."

Her shoulders sink and she stares at me for a moment. As hard-shelled as Nikki is, she has a soft side. "That's horrible for them to say."

I shrug. "They're not wrong. With age comes a decline in reflexes, and I'm already nursing so many injuries from previous fights."

"How old are you?"

"You mean you haven't Googled me yet?" I raise an eyebrow.

She shakes her head. I'm surprised.

"I'm thirty-four. You?"

"Twenty-nine and thirty-four is not *old*. Look at you." Her eyes fall down my body.

I like when she looks at me like that. I know she likes what she sees. If only we could get over this barrier, which reminds me...

"Tell me now why you don't believe in love."

She rolls her eyes, which says she was hoping I wouldn't remember. "My dad cheated on my mom. I caught him and had to be the one who told my mom."

Well, shit. That could definitely mess someone up. "How old were you?"

"Fourteen. I was with my friends at the movies. It was one of the old theaters and they were playing nineties movies. We were walking up the aisle and laughing at this disgusting couple making out in the back row. One of my friends yelled, 'Get a room,' and they stopped. But when the guy turned around, it was my dad."

I'm speechless. That's harsh. "What did your dad do?"

"He tried to talk to me, but I screamed and told him to get away from me. My friend's mom picked us up from the movies and drove me home. All my friends kept wanting to talk about it and ask me how I was doing. I just wanted to go to my room and forget it all. But instead, I had to break my mom's heart and tell her what I saw. I'll never forget the look on her face." Nikki sucks in a ragged breath.

"I'm sorry. That truly sucks."

She nods and puts the plate of potato skins back on the table. "I'll eat all of this if I'm not careful."

"Stress eater?" I ask.

"Emotional eater."

"Thanks for trusting me," I say because I'm not sure what else to say, but I do feel honored that she told me.

"You trusted me and you're in a worse position than I am if I let out your secrets." A nervous laugh leaks out of her.

"True. But I know it's hard for you to share."

She nods. "My dad was everything to me, but I should've known. You have no idea how many times I've had to console my friends in high school and college after their boyfriends cheated on them. Temptation wins time and time again."

"That's not always true."

She looks at me. "So you're celibate?"

I laugh, but she's serious. "No, but I'm not always looking to hook up. Hell, I married you the first night we met. What does that tell you?"

"That you probably shouldn't drink tequila again."

I grin. "Ah, I think I make good decisions when I drink tequila. Look at us now."

She scoffs. "Yeah, living a fairy tale fake relationship."

"Well, at least we're having fun." The words sound hollow, and I wish I could take them back. I'm having more than fun with her. I haven't been part of a relationship in a long time, and I forgot how good it feels.

Then again, I have to be wary, because so many of those old friends and girlfriends were in it for what I could give them. They liked the fame and the cameras and the money. Nikki doesn't seem that way, which is what intrigues me, but I haven't always been a good judge of character.

"True. Thanks for tonight. I had a great time. The show was spectacular." She gets up and grabs a bottle of water.

"Where are you going?"

"I'm going to go to bed now."

Way to go, Stone, you ruined the conversation by bringing up her dad.

"Are you sure? We could watch a movie or something?"

She yawns. "No. I'm beat. Thank you again."

"You're welcome."

Our eyes lock for a moment, then both of our gazes skim

down the other. If she was anyone else, I'd break the distance and kiss her until she begged me to take her to bed. But she's far from ready to admit there might be something more than just a fake marriage here.

"Good night," she says softly.

"'Night, Nikki."

I watch her disappear down the small hallway toward her room, happy that at least some progress was made tonight.

Chapter Eleven

"Oh boy, hold on. This is going to get bumpy now"
~Nikki Greene

Nikki

"Did you sleep well?" Logan asks as we step out of his suite and head down the hallway toward the elevators.

"I did."

"Happy to be going home?" We enter the elevator, and he presses the button for the main floor.

"Yep, except for the part where the interview will air and everyone will be talking about it."

"Gossip bothers you, yet you host a gossip show on a radio station?" He chuckles.

"I never make anything up, it's all the truth."

He grows somber and stares at me. "That's important to you? Truth?"

"It's the reason I do what I do. Lies spread faster than truth. I get the truth out there before the lies spread."

He stares at me so intensely, I shift my weight. "Why?"

I don't want to get into what happens once your family has imploded and you find yourselves the subject of rumors and lies, so I say, "Exactly what I said. Lies spread faster and do more damage than the truth."

He doesn't ask any more questions—probably because I put the iron gate down—and the silence of the small space soon gets interrupted by the sounds and bells from the casino floor. Just like he did on the way in, Logan takes my hand and leads me through the throngs of slot machines to get us outside before anyone can stop us.

We're just about to the doors when a petite brunette steps in front of him. "Log?" she says, but not in a tone that makes me think it's a coincidence she ran into us.

"Melanie?"

So he knows her name. Something in my gut says I won't like what's about to happen.

"I heard you were in town." Her gaze detours down to where our hands are joined. I move to remove mine, but Logan grips tighter.

"Yeah, I'm here with Nikki." He looks at me. "My wife."

Melanie laughs and her curly hair bounces up and down. "I heard something about a drunk Vegas wedding." Her gaze zeroes in on me. "You can't be serious?"

"As serious as a married couple," Logan says. "Nikki, this is Melanie."

I'd offer my hand, but Melanie crosses her arms and her breasts practically pop out from how low cut her shirt is.

"Can we talk?" She lowers her voice, but I hear someone to our right say Logan's name.

I turn and a group of guys are pointing and looking up things on their phone.

"I gotta go. We have a flight to catch." Logan steps us around her.

"You're just going to walk away from me?" Melanie says

in a loud enough voice that it's clear she wants everyone in the vicinity to hear her. "*Logan Stone!*"

Logan releases my hand and walks back over to her, leaving me by the door. The group of guys are now pointing at me and whispering to one another. A woman snaps a picture, and soon a small horseshoe forms around us.

Logan lowers his voice, his mouth right to Melanie's ear, and she glares at me from over his shoulder. When I'm about to leave the casino and hop in a cab, Logan walks away from her and comes to me, grabbing my hand one more time and guiding me outside to a black SUV, ignoring the pleas from onlookers for a signature.

Once we're away from the hotel and on our way to the airport, he turns to me. "I'm sorry. Melanie is an ex, but I haven't been with her in a long time."

"But she knew this is where you stay?"

"She knows I stay wherever an upcoming fight is. Yes."

"It's none of my business. It's fine."

He takes my hand. "I want you to know she's no one."

I nod. "Whatever, we both have exes."

I assume he has a lot more than me, since I don't really date because dating is generally going somewhere and I usually sabotage my relationships before they get too serious.

"Let's get home to Sunrise Bay." He leans his head back on the seat and blows out a long breath.

I'm thinking Melanie was a little more than a typical ex, but I'm not going to ask. My gut says I won't like the answer he gives.

WE BOTH FELL asleep on the plane ride—which I'm thankful for, because I'm quite done with talking for a while. Back in Sunrise Bay, the usual SUV pulls up to my house and I catch sight of Rylan across the street, playing soccer out front of Hank and my mom's house.

"Hey, Ry!" I scream and wave.

He stops playing and I figure I might as well introduce my half-brother to his brother-in-law.

"Who's that?" Logan asks.

"My little brother. Come on." We cross the street as Rylan bounces the soccer ball from knee to knee. "Rylan, this is Logan—"

"Stone?" he asks, his eyes huge. "Jed said something, but I didn't believe him. You really married Logan Stone?"

I roll my eyes.

Logan puts out his arm between us. "Nice to meet you. You're a soccer guy, huh?"

I ruffle Rylan's brown hair. "He's the best in the area. At least the best boy in the area." I give him a teasing smile because he practices with a girl from Lake Starlight who's really good as well. We're always razzing him about liking her. He swears he doesn't.

"I'm the best," Rylan says. "I beat Calista yesterday."

"Calista?" Logan asks.

"Calista is Rylan's practice partner."

Rylan backs away from me. He's growing too old for me to show affection now. "She's annoying."

Logan looks at me with a knowing look like he understands what's going on. Twelve-year-olds are complicated individuals. Almost a teenager, but not quite.

"Girls have cooties," Logan says, and Rylan's eyebrows scrunch at me.

I wrap my arms around Rylan, and he tries to get away.

"I'm spreading my cooties all over you. Admit it. You like her."

Rylan squirms out of my hold and runs away, kicking his soccer ball.

"Nice to meet you!" Logan calls to him.

Rylan turns around, running backward. "Come to one of my games. My teammates would never believe my sister got drunk and married Logan Stone."

I narrow my eyes as Rylan laughs, running into the house, but just as he disappears inside, my mom steps out.

"Hey, you two," Mom says and walks out to us barefoot. Her feet must be freezing. It's not that warm out yet.

"Oh boy, hold on. This is going to get bumpy now," I murmur.

"You guys are back from Vegas?" she asks, coming to my side and running her hand down my arm, silently asking if everything went well.

"We are," I say.

"I just saw the interview."

Of course she did.

"And?" Logan asks. "How did we look?"

My mom beams at me. "You look in love."

But she's questioning me with her eyes. I hate that my mom always knows everything. She probably knows this is all fake.

Logan rushes to my side and puts his arm around my waist. "Because we are."

My mom smiles, but it doesn't reach her eyes. "What else did you two do?"

"We went to dinner and Cirque du Soleil. The show was amazing. You and Hank should go sometime."

She glances back at the house. "Yeah, maybe we'll get away sometime. So!" She claps her hands. "I'm thinking dinner? When can we have you guys over and get to know our son-in-law better?"

I slide closer to Logan. "He's on a special diet. Has to train."

I made up the excuse so he doesn't feel obligated. Surely dinner with my mom will come with an interrogation. By the time dessert is served, she'll be acting as though she just solved the case. Not to mention this is all pretend. Why would he want to go on a get-to-know-my-family mission?

"You can tell me what to cook," she says, staring only at Logan.

"Please don't go to any trouble for me," he says.

She waves him off. "You're part of the family now. It'd be my pleasure."

"We'll let you know." I plead with my eyes for her to stop asking.

"How about Sunday?" She looks between the two of us hopefully.

"Mom, he's not ready for the entire family yet."

She smiles and I know that she's not going to accept no as an answer. "A big MMA fighter can't handle a big family?" Again, she puts her sole attention on Logan.

"It's no problem. Sunday should be great," he says, smiling as though he might actually mean it.

She claps again. "Then it's settled. Around three work?"

I groan and Logan chuckles. "Sounds good."

"See you then, Mom." I slide my hand in Logan's to walk back over to my house.

"Hey, Nik, give me a call when you get some time," she says.

"Sure thing." I smile and wave.

But I have no plans of calling her. She's only going to figure out what Logan and I are doing, then I'll have to hear the speech again about my dad and how not all men are horrible disappointments, just look at Hank, Jed, and my stepbrothers, there are good men out in the world.

I'm not in the mood.

We reach the bottom of the hill and Logan stops at the sidewalk. "You okay with that?"

I look back and see my mom is on the porch, watching us. I make a mental note to tell her how creepy she looks doing that. "You know that whole question game we played last night?"

His face grows serious. "Yeah."

"Tonight we're playing fast five, because if we're going to fool everyone into thinking we're madly in love, we have to fool Marla Greene first. She's our harshest critic."

"Bring it on." He smiles.

Sometimes I think he likes what's going on with us. That he wants us to be more. He didn't have to do all that yesterday for me—the show and expensive dinner. But the thought that he's doing it because he wants something more gives me butterflies. I have to make sure that feeling dies. Otherwise, I might as well hand him my heart now and watch him smash it into smithereens against the concrete.

"Then let's get my stuff moved into the Linville house and make up some flashcards."

"Don't you think that's a bit much?" he asks.

I stop with my key in the lock of my house. "Not when it comes to my mom. She's going to dig deep. Believe me."

He laughs as we step into the house I share with my sisters, but he has no idea. Marla Greene missed her calling as a police detective. Or her motherly intuition and skills are just fine-tuned. Regardless, she's already sniffing around, which means I'm too transparent.

Game on.

Chapter Twelve

Logan

Iknew my time alone with Nikki would come to an end, but it came crashing down when my team arrived an hour ago. Luckily, she's at the radio station. The chef has overtaken the kitchen, and my team of trainers is settling in the back guest house. Right now, I'm thankful Vince decided to stay down in Vegas and come up in a month or so to make sure we're staying on track. He has his own feelings in regard to this marriage with Nikki, and I don't care to have him around.

My head trainer, Craig, walks in as I'm discussing with the chef, Iris, what Nikki likes. "Sugar with her coffee," I say, and she nods, putting away some key ingredients she brought with her. The entire group seems to think I moved them to Greenland and they won't be able to get anything up here.

"I figured we'd go for a run," Craig says, stretching.

"You just got in. What the hell?"

"There's a gym in town I want to check out. See if we can

make an arrangement with them to get in there." He rotates his head. "Come on. You're on a time crunch and need to get started. You've been having fun long enough."

"Fun?" I ask.

He punches me in the shoulder. "Bedroom exercise doesn't count, you know that." He laughs.

Iris shakes her head. "You two can leave my kitchen now."

I stand from the stool. Craig is right though. I need to get my ass in gear. "I'm picking up Nikki after work."

"Man, you've got it bad." He walks out, still stretching his arms. "I'll be outside."

He leaves the house and I put on my shoes before joining him. Usually no one has to push me to work out, but lately, all I want to do is sit around and heal from the last fight. I won't tell anyone, but Garcia gave me a run for my money.

Craig and I start off with a jog, but it quickly turns into a run and I realize way too late he's mapped out all of Sunrise Bay. The fucker took me the long way to town and up every hill.

"We're gonna have to do a lot more cardio this time. You were fading too fast with Garcia," he says.

"I know. The guy has the energy of a puppy."

"And Rinaldo isn't a sleeping twelve-year-old basset hound either. So get ready for lots of running. We'll be concentrating a lot of our effort there at first." He pats my stomach and runs up the hill, turning around to egg me on.

"Please, you can't beat me." I run up and past him, continuing on the path.

He quickly catches up. "I have to say, I never thought I'd see the day you'd get married."

I glance over, then set my eyes on the downtown area that's coming up. "Why do you say that?"

"You never seemed much interested in it. I thought for a while maybe with Melanie, but after she quit her job and started playing those games with the media, I hoped you wouldn't."

I definitely dodged a bullet with Melanie.

"It just kind of happened." I'm not lying. Nikki seemed to drop into my life at the best possible time.

He pats me on the back. "I'm happy for you. I saw your interview with Rick and you both seem very into one another."

I smile, thinking about how close we were on the couch. Her hand on my thigh and my arm around her shoulders. The way she'd look up at me to answer a question and then have a soft smile on her lips afterward. "Yeah. You'll meet her in a few."

We finish our run and slow down to a walk as we reach the town square from one of the parking lot entrances.

"I see these cobblestone streets and I think where the hell are we?" Craig laughs.

"Crazy, right?"

Craig leads the way to a place called Pump It Up, and I quirk an eyebrow as he opens the door.

"This is the best I can do without us going into Anchorage. You picked here, remember?" He pats me on the back, and we step into the gym.

"Logan," a guy says. As he gets closer, I notice it's Jed, Nikki's brother. He puts out his hand. "Are you gonna work out here?"

He's sweaty and I wonder what the hell he does for a living that he can work out midday. Oh yeah, he owns the brewery, I think.

"Are you the owner?" Craig interrupts.

"No, this is Nikki's brother, Jed," I say. "Jed, this is Craig, one of my trainers."

Craig puts out his hand and they shake. "Try, *the* trainer."

I shake my head because I have more than one trainer, but Craig would be the lead trainer if that was actually a title.

"Nice to meet you. The owner is Trent. He's in the office." Jed points us in the right direction.

"Thanks." Craig heads to the office.

"You like it here?" I ask Jed.

He runs a towel down his face. "I do, but it's not like there're other options either."

I nod, looking at the equipment. It appears on the old side. Plus, I'm gonna need a ring if I really want to make sure my sparring stays in place.

"You're probably thinking right now about how my sister moved you to the sticks." Jed laughs. "I get it. We lived in Arizona before we came up here and I was like, 'What kind of place is this?' But it grows on you."

I nod, staring at the pathetic gym. For the first time, I wonder what my long game here is. Do I think I'm going to live here forever if this thing with Nikki works out? Surely I can't live here permanently and still fight. My wheels are turning, but I stop them before I get ahead of myself. There's a high probability that in three months, I'll be leaving as a divorced man.

"Nah, I love this town." Except for right now when I realize that not all my training requirements are at my disposal.

Craig comes out with who I suspect is Trent. He's a taller guy, in his thirties, and from the belly that strains over the waistband of his pants, doesn't look like he actively uses his gym.

"This is Logan Stone," Craig introduces me, and I shake Trent's hand.

"Nice to meet you," I say.

Trent crosses his arms. "So your buddy says you're a big fighter. You're the one who married Nikki Greene?"

"He's my new brother-in-law." Jed winks then smiles at me. "You missed your opportunity, Trent."

Trent tilts his head, giving Jed a disgruntled expression. Is this one of Nikki's exes?

"Did you date my girl?" I ask because why fuck around? I meant it when I told Nikki I don't play games.

"Ah... once, but it was just coffee."

"Technically, it was a book reading and coffee was served. Nikki and Trent shared a table, right?" Jed continues.

"Yeah," Trent admits with his head down. "She said she didn't do relationships."

"Well, she doesn't. She married Logan the same night she met him." Jed laughs, and when I don't, he's quick to walk toward the free weights. "I'll be over there if you need me."

I walk around the gym, Craig following. "What are you thinking?"

"Honestly, the guy's got more space than he needs. I say we offer to rent out a section. Put up a ring. We can get you weights back at the house, but if you want to get your own here, we could do that too."

I nod as Craig maps out what he's thinking. Though I've given some thought to retiring from fighting, if I did choose to, I'd be disappointing everyone on my team. I'm amazed every day by how dedicated they are to my success. I know that's rare in this business. I'll have to make sure they all land in a good place whenever I do call it quits.

"Okay, let's do it," I say. It's not ideal, but I'm confident we can figure out a way to make it work.

I didn't really need to see this place. I trust Craig to make the decision on his own, but I like that I'll be working out close to where Nikki works.

"All right, I'll go work my magic." Craig goes back to speak with Trent.

I pull out my phone and text Nikki.

> When are you off?

In about ten minutes. Just in a meeting.

> Wait for me. I'm coming to get you.

No need. I'm good.

> Did I put a question mark in my last text?

Do you really think that bossy tone is going to work on me?

> :P No, just testing the waters.

So??

> So what?

I'm waiting for a please

> PLEASE let me come and pick you up.

Fine. We should make an appearance together anyway.

> Be there in fifteen.

I don't like to wait.

I click the screen off on my phone and pocket it.

Craig comes over and slaps me on the back. "Sold. We have to move their gym equipment over to the other area, but it's ours. I texted the guys and they're coming here today."

"Perfect. And the ring?"

"Should be here in three days and we can start assembling it."

"Man, a smart person hired you." I smack him on the back, and we head out of the place. "See you, Jed."

"One piece of advice," Jed calls. "I heard Ethel and Dori were looking for you. Something about you teaching a self-defense class at their retirement place."

"Who's that?" Craig asks.

"Nikki's grandma and her friend," I say.

"And I'm telling you this because you're new here," Jed says. "That place isn't like any retirement home you've ever been to, so I'd dodge it if you're able."

"Thanks. I'll remember that."

We leave Pump It Up and I say goodbye to Craig to go over and meet Nikki. She's waiting outside, sitting on a bench and looking at her phone.

I slyly sit down next to her. "How is my wife today?"

She glances at me and laughs. "She's tired and needs a foot rub."

"Well then, let's get you home so I can handle my husbandly duties."

She stands and puts her bag over her shoulder. I take it from her. "I was just kidding about the foot rub."

"Hey, this might not be real, but this is how'd I be if I were your real husband." I swing her bag over my shoulder and entwine our hands to walk down the street.

"You'd be a nice husband then." She tips her head toward the street that will take us to the Linville house.

"By the way, the team is here, and Iris wants to know what you want her to stock."

"Stock? And who is Iris?"

"She's our cook, and she wants to know what your staples are. What you like to eat."

Nikki shakes her head. "Man, marrying you comes with perks girls only dream about."

Isn't that every woman's first impression? But I want Nikki to want to stay married to me for me, not the perks that come with me.

Chapter Thirteen

Nikki

Sunday at three sharp, we walk into my mom and Hank's house. I already know Cade and Adam are here from the trucks parked in the driveway. I shouldn't have been so naive to think she wouldn't invite more people. It's classic Mom.

"Mom!" I yell as we slip off our shoes and our coats. Logan, ever the gentleman I'm discovering, helps me with mine. We hang them on the coat rack and walk farther into the house.

Glancing into the living room, I see chairs situated in groups of two and I groan.

"What?" Logan asks.

"Let's just hope my assumptions are wrong."

"Okay." He laughs, but he doesn't know. He's not used to this family. I know my mom has some sort of game planned.

As I expected, Mom is busy in the kitchen. Cade and Adam are watching a baseball game, and Presley and Lucy are snacking on the appetizers. Hank is outside by the grill.

"Hello," I say.

Presley and Lucy come over and hug me, then shake Logan's hand.

My mom wipes her hands on a dishtowel and rounds the counter to hug Logan and me. "So happy you both could make it."

"Can you explain the living room to me?" I whisper in her ear.

"Later, sweetie." She pats my hand and goes back to preparing a ginormous salad. "So, Logan, I had no idea what to serve you, so I did a little research."

I sigh and Logan laughs, running his hand down my lower back. We'll just ignore the fact I stepped into him because I find myself cherishing the times when we act like a real couple.

"I'm flexible," he says. "Whatever I eat tonight, I just have to be that much harder on myself tomorrow."

"Well, I'm sure my daughter didn't tell you, but I make salad dressings. I did a little digging on you and found out you're a ranch lover but can't take the calories."

"Where did you read that?" I ask. I haven't had the guts to Google Logan because I'm afraid of what I'll find out. Even if we're not a real couple, I have to pretend we are for the next several months.

Mom beams. "I have my sources."

Hank comes inside with a platter of grilled chicken. "Hey, you two." He puts the plate down and shakes Logan's hand, then kisses me on the cheek. "I was just watching this segment on you fighting Rinaldo."

Logan nods. "He's favored right now."

I put my arm through his arm. "You'll win. I know it."

Logan looks at me, and the way his blue eyes almost smile at me makes my heart sing. "Thanks."

I divert my gaze when I realize we've been staring at one another too long and find my mom scrutinizing us.

"Okay, dinner, guys," Mom says, and we all file into the dining room.

Cade and Adam come by, saying hello to Logan and me.

"Tell me about the living room, boys?" I plead.

Cade holds up his hands. "I don't know. I plan on sneaking out after the meal."

"Where's Rylan?" Logan asks.

"He's at a friend's house," Hank says. "We figured adults only."

I sit in my seat and Adam sits next to me, Lucy sitting across from him.

"Logan and I can separate," I offer, standing.

"No way, you guys are the newest couple. I know how we were when we first got married." Adam pats my shoulder. I'd swear my mom set him up to say that.

"Here's the fettuccini alfredo." A big plate of pasta is put in the middle of the table. "I have chicken, shrimp, or meatballs. Whichever you prefer." Mom disappears into the kitchen, then returns with the bowl of salad. I expect her to put it on the side of the table for all of us to share, but she places it right in front of Logan. "So, greens. I added a lot of vegetables in there, like squash and some black beans. Hank, do you have the plate?"

"Got it." He holds it up, six chicken breasts on the damn thing.

Mom takes the plate from Hank and sets it down next to Logan. "I didn't put in any seasoning because it said that was a no-no. That you wouldn't want to retain any water."

Logan swallows hard, staring at all the food Mom clearly expects him to eat.

"Oh, and just in case you don't like the ranch, I made

you a sampler of all my salad dressings." She sets six small jars in front of his huge bowl of salad.

"Mom, he's not going to eat all this," I say.

Logan's hand lands on my thigh under the table and a jolt of arousal runs up my leg. "Thank you so much, Marla. I appreciate it."

Mom smiles.

As she heads into the kitchen again, I whisper, "I'm sorry."

He squeezes my thigh. "Don't be. It's a nice gesture."

Logan cuts up his chicken and tries every dressing, commenting on them to my mom. He's sweet and endearing, and even though Cade and Adam asked him question after question about fights and how he heals, he never seemed to grow tired of them.

For a moment when Logan swung his arm around my shoulders in a carefree way, I forgot it was all a farce. Whoever does actually land Logan Stone will be a lucky lady. Too bad I'm not her.

AFTER DINNER, Mom looks at Hank. "We're going to have dessert in the living room."

Here we go. I can't even imagine what's about to happen.

I sigh. "What are we doing?"

My mom gives me her impatient-with-my-attitude expression. "Since Cade and Presley are about to be married, and Adam and Lucy just renewed their vows, and you and Logan are married, Hank and I thought it would be fun to play the Newlywed Game."

I'm barely able to keep my head up when she says it. My neck wants to give out and let my forehead hit the table.

She's got to be kidding me. This is her way of toying with us and trying to find out whether we've actually connected after our impromptu marriage.

"Mom," I say, but she ignores me.

"This will be fun," Logan says.

I look at him as if he's crazy. But at least we did the whole question round thing the other day after my mom suggested this dinner.

"We'll do the guys first, so you girls hang out in here."

I give Mom a wane smile.

Cade kisses Presley bye and Adam kisses Lucy. I stare at Logan, unsure what to do. All this time, our lips haven't been on one another's since that first night. Sadly, I don't even remember it. I bet it was a great kiss.

Logan dips down, and I look from the corner of my eye to see my family staring. At the last minute, I turn and his lips land on my cheek.

"You know how I feel about public displays of affection," I say to play it off.

A satisfactory grin forms on my mom's lips as she watches us. Damn it.

Mom, Hank, and the guys go into the living room as the girls refill their wine glasses.

"So, give us all the details," Lucy says, leaning over the table.

"What details?" I ask.

"He seems so sweet. I mean, to eat almost the entire plate of chicken? He's probably going to throw up." Presley eyes the plate with only a half breast left and the majority of his salad.

In order to dodge their questions, I figure I'll clean up the table, but they follow me.

"So it's real? Like you're really happy and trying to stay married to him?" Presley asks.

I want to tell her it's quiet time now, but instead, I lie. "Yep."

"I love it. I mean, it's so romantic." Lucy swoons.

Presley looks at Lucy. "Romantic?"

Lucy shrugs. "Maybe romantic is the wrong word, but to meet someone and marry them the same night? So impromptu and—"

"So not you," Presley says to me. She's not wrong, even if she's known me for less time than anyone in this house. Well, except for my husband. "That's why I couldn't be happier you took a chance and it's paying off. Love can be scary." She runs her hand down my arm.

"*Girls!*" Hank yells at the best time.

We abandon the dishes to join the guys. When we enter the living room, all the guys are in one chair of the pairings and we each sit beside our man. I'm probably going to embarrass myself and get every question wrong.

"Okay, the guys have written down their answers to the questions. Now I'll ask you ladies how you think they would answer." Mom acts as if she's really a game show host. She lives for this stuff. "First question, what is your spouse's guilty pleasure?"

Luckily she starts with Adam on the far end, so I have a little time to think about it. Lucy answers right, and so does Presley. Each couple high fives and hugs. Then my mom's eyes are on me.

"Ho Hos." I squint one eye because he could have been lying to me that night in Vegas.

Logan holds up his card and it says Ho Hos.

"Yay!" I hug him and his arms wrap around me. God, he smells good. I quickly back away.

"Next question, and we'll start with you, Nikki. How did you know your spouse was the one?" Hank asks this time.

"After the fourth tequila shot?" Adam says sarcastically. I narrow my eyes and he laughs while Lucy hits him in the stomach. "Come on. You can't get drunk-married in Vegas and expect people not to make fun of it."

The only thing I'm happy about is that Adam's teasing gives me time to think of what Logan would say. I have no idea and I'm assuming he doesn't know either, so I'm just gonna have to guess. "Because he was good-looking?"

Logan holds up his card. "'Because she trusted me,'" he says, reading his answer.

"Trusted you?" I ask.

Logan shrugs. "I don't think you've told a lot of people about the podcast thing. The fact you felt like you could tell me meant something."

"Podcast?" Cade asks. "Are you leaving the station? Thank God."

I roll my eyes. "No. I'm not leaving the radio station."

"One day she will. When her podcast is successful," Logan says, squeezing my thigh.

I place my hand on his and mouth, "Thank you." Who would guess a guy like him could be so sweet?

The questions go on, and although we get all the generic questions right, the other couples beat us on the sentimental stuff. Adam and Lucy win, which is no surprise. They've known one another since they were six.

As Logan and I are leaving for the night, my mom says, "Rylan wanted you guys to come to his game next weekend. Are you available?"

"Yeah, we'd love to go," Logan answers before I can politely decline.

"Great. It's Saturday."

Logan's head falls back. "What time? I'm getting my mom from the airport."

My head twists in his direction. Did he just say *his mom*?

"You look like you didn't know, Nikki," my mom says.

I force a smile. "Of course I knew. It just slipped my mind. You can meet us there afterward," I say through gritted teeth to Logan.

I knew nothing about his mom coming. Where is she going to stay? In the house with us? If so, does that mean I can't sleep in another room? Why didn't he tell me this earlier?

So many questions and no answers. I suppose it doesn't matter though, because no matter what, this changes everything. If she stays with us, we'll have to act like a couple at home too.

Chapter Fourteen

Logan

The first time I've driven myself in Alaska is today, when I'm picking up my mom from the airport in Anchorage. The freedom of being by myself in the SUV is nice, and I use the drive to reflect. I do more of that while I'm waiting for her to come out of the airport. I think about Nikki and what's happening between us. Every time I feel as if we're getting closer, she pulls back.

This past week, Iris made us dinner every night, but after our meal, Nikki would usually head upstairs and I'd go get another workout. This isn't what I'd hoped for when it came to us. I had hopes that we'd grow closer, and if I'm being honest with myself, that she'd fall in love with me. But that doesn't seem to be happening.

My mom walks out of the airport and I rush out of the vehicle, eager to get out of my own head and feelings. I'm not usually like this, but Nikki's got a hold on me like no one ever has.

"Hey, Mom," I say and hug her.

"My baby boy." She draws back and looks me over. "Too skinny. I can't wait for you to retire and look like a normal person."

This is typical of my mom. I'm not sure she likes my career choice, although she's never told me so. I'm afraid to ask.

"I'm not looking to retire for some time," I tell her, though we both know that's not the truth.

"Where's my daughter-in-law?" she asks, handing me her suitcase. I put it in the back and we both round the SUV, climbing in.

"She's at her brother's soccer game." I buckle my seat belt and shift the vehicle into drive.

"Oh, so I get to meet the entire family already?" Her excitement is bubbling over. This is my mom, Miss Personality. Everyone is her friend.

"I can drop you off at the house."

"No way, I'm excited to meet everyone." She crosses her legs and relaxes, staring out the window. "It's so beautiful here. Have you seen a moose?"

I laugh. "Not yet. A black bear though."

Her mouth drops open.

"Kidding. But Craig keeps taking me on these trails, and I'm fairly sure I'm gonna be a bear's meal one day."

"I'm going to have to talk to Craig. So, how are things going?" She shifts in her seat to face me.

I haven't told my mom about Nikki's and my arrangement yet. I haven't even told Nikki that my mom knows our relationship isn't close to being real, and that Nikki left me the next morning. "Could be better?"

"Meaning?" she says, tipping her head so she can see my eyes. She's always said they speak to her more than the words that come out of my mouth.

"I made an arrangement with her." Why beat around the bush? My mom will figure it out shortly anyway.

"Arrangement?"

"Why are you talking in one-word sentences?"

"Because my son is trying to lie to me. Unsuccessfully, I might add. What did you do?"

I'm driving, so I can still dodge her a little longer, but she's the only one I trust to tell me if I'm wasting my time with Nikki. Maybe I'm seeing things that aren't really there. "I asked her to pretend to be happily married so that the press would stay off my back until the fight."

"Log." Her tone is one of disapproval. The tone I hate the most when it comes to my mom.

"She wasn't very receptive to the whole 'my gut tells me we might have something here' thing." I sound like a pathetic lovesick loser.

"And why did she agree to pretend?"

I'm quiet for a moment, but she makes a sound to say she's waiting on my answer.

"I agreed to get five celebrities to do the podcast she wants to start."

"Interesting. I thought after Melanie, we agreed that we didn't want women who liked the idea of your money more than you?"

The last person I want to talk about is Melanie.

"If by *us* you mean *me*, yes, but she's doing me a favor and I'm doing one for her. It has nothing to do with money." I get off the highway.

"Still. You deserve a woman who wants you for what's inside."

"You make it sound like all I have to go on is my personality. I might not be a model, but I'm not that hard on the eyes."

We stop at a light and she puts her hand on my cheek to turn my face toward her. "Logan, you're more than easy on the eyes. I mean hello, I'm your mother."

I laugh. "Nikki doesn't much care for my career choice."

Someone honks and I shift my attention back to the road.

"Not many people like to watch their loved ones get beat up. Can't say I blame her."

"I think it's more than that. I think it might be the fame and the... women." After hearing the story of her dad and how many times she's accused me of sleeping around, that's the conclusion I've come to. Anyone who has issues with faithfulness in a relationship wouldn't want to be married to a man who has women throwing themselves at him all the time. She believes no man can withstand sex when it's offered to them, regardless of who's doing the offering.

"That makes sense. You have a lot of opportunity," Mom says.

"Opportunities I rarely take."

"True." She's quiet for a minute. "And what does Vince say about her?"

I pull into the sports complex, park, and sit for a moment. "He's not happy. You know him. Worried about me preparing for this fight and..."

She rolls her eyes. "Please tell me this isn't about that bullshit you can't be with someone and still win a fight?"

"You know last time I was with someone I lost. So if I'm with Nikki at the fight, then—"

She throws her hands in the air. "Then nothing. You know I believe in signs, but that one is superstition and stupidity. You deserve to be happy, Logan."

"I'm not sure she sees all the great qualities in me that you do." I chuckle.

"I saw the interview. She seems sweet, and I liked the way she glows when she looks at you."

"It's all an act, Mom." There have been times over the past week when I thought maybe she was feeling something, especially after the dinner at her mom's, but I must've been wrong since she hasn't spent one night hanging out with me all week.

She opens her door. "I guess we'll see about that."

I fly out of the SUV. "What does that mean?"

"You know me, I have a sense about these things. I'll be able to tell if she's playing you or not."

I catch up to my mom. "Her entire family will probably be here, so don't question her in front of everyone."

"Oh, give me some credit." She opens the door of the sports complex and heads in.

I take a deep, cleansing breath, hoping she doesn't embarrass me.

We walk in and there are parents everywhere. I spot Marla and Hank and I'm about to approach them to introduce them to my mother, but Ethel steps in front of us.

"Logan," Ethel says and wraps her arms around my waist. "Good to see you."

"Is this Nikki?" my mom jokes.

Ethel looks at her. "Who are you?"

"Ethel, this is my mom, Pauline. This is Nikki's grandma, Ethel."

"Pleasure to meet you," my mom says. They shake hands.

"And this is my friend, Dori. Her great-granddaughter plays with my grandson, Rylan," Ethel says of the blue-haired woman who's always hanging around her.

My mom gushes hellos and can't stop smiling.

"Did you talk to Logan?" Dori asks Ethel, and I remember what Jed told me at Pump It Up.

"You know what? My mom's dying to meet Nikki. We should go." I urge my mom away by placing my hand on the small of her back and ushering her to start walking.

"She's not here yet." Dori steps in front of my mom. "Probably getting all done up for you."

Doubtful.

"We were talking to our community director at the retirement home, and some of us are feeling unsafe around the area," Ethel says.

"Is there a lot of crime around here?" my mom asks.

"Oh no. Well, I mean, we're old, so it doesn't take much," Dori chimes in.

"Logan could help you with some moves." My mom looks at me. "Teach them some self-defense tactics."

"I appreciate you thinking of me, but I can't be throwing any of you over my shoulder or back. I'm not sure I'm the right person."

As for Nikki, I'd love to show her a move or two.

"Nonsense. We can't trust just anyone, and you're a professional. You'd be doing a great favor to the people of Northern Lights Retirement." Ethel gives me a look. If I had a grandma, I'd never be able to say no to that look.

"Oh, he'll do it." My mom pats my stomach. "Tell these sweet ladies you'll do it."

I give my mom a look to tell her to stay out of this, but what choice do I have at this point? These three women will hate me—and I suspect they won't stop pestering me—if I don't agree to this. "Sure."

Dori punches me in the arm. "I knew you'd agree."

This should be fun. "Can't wait."

"I'm going to go call everyone." Dori walks away but is quickly swallowed up by a group of small kids.

"Those are her great-grandkids. Did you know that I don't have any great-grandkids yet?" Ethel says to me. "I'm sick of not having anything to brag about at the retirement home. Do you get what I'm saying?" She nudges me with her elbow.

"She wants you and Nikki to have kids, Log," my mom fills me in as though I can't figure it out on my own.

"I get what she's saying," I say to my mom, annoyed over how this entire conversation is going.

"Don't worry, I understand you can't be using all your energy to get Nikki knocked up right now. After the fight, I'll really start putting the pressure on. Which reminds me, Earl wanted to know if you have a bookie down in Vegas. He wants to make a wager."

I shake my head as my mom laughs. I say, "Let me get some names for Earl."

Rylan runs over to our little group. "Coach said you can sit on the bench with us so people don't bombard you with questions. Want to?"

I look at my mom.

Ethel slides her arm through my mom's. "See an old woman to the bleachers?"

My mom smiles and nods for me to go ahead with Rylan. "Ethel and I will be in the stands. Good luck."

"Pass Calista the ball like a good boy," Ethel says.

I hear Rylan blow out a breath as I follow him toward the field. "My coach was a professional soccer player, and he says he knows what it's like with the moms and stuff. Plus, he knows Grandma and Dori can be a handful. Figured if you really want to watch my game, you'd need to be on our bench."

"Oh really?" I bite my lip to stop from grinning. This kid is cute.

Rylan runs onto the field, and his teammate kicks the ball to him and Rylan kicks it in the net. I sit on the bench, loving the up-close look but wishing I could sit next to Nikki. Especially since my mom is over there unsupervised. Who knows what will come out of her mouth?

Chapter Fifteen

Nikki

Molly and I walk into the sports complex where Rylan plays soccer. We're a little late because Molly changed her outfit so many times. She's never been this concerned when going to Rylan's games, but she hardly ever attends them.

We walk over to the bleacher my entire family has taken over. I have no idea how Rylan handles all of us cheering for him while other players have one or two parents here. Then again, the Baileys from Lake Starlight are a big group. The only time I see Dori and Ethel not sitting side by side are at these games.

I scan the bleachers for Logan because he said he'd be here after picking up his mom, but there's no sign of him.

"Sit down guys," Adam says.

We slide into the bottom bleacher because the game has started and Rylan has the ball.

"Will he just pass it to Calista? She's wide open," Mom mumbles to herself.

She's right, but Rylan is a ball hog and dodges right and left toward the net.

"That's your grandson?" a woman asks, and I turn to see someone I don't know sitting with Ethel.

"Yep. And see that girl in the braids? He likes her."

"Mom," Hank says.

"What? We all know it. He's twelve, dear. When you were twelve, you were taking long showers."

"Can we please not do this here?" Cade asks. "We embarrass the kid enough."

"Isn't that the truth. A twelve-year-old's alone time isn't something to joke about." Jed laughs.

Molly says, "I think a thirty-two-year-old's alone time isn't something to joke about." Her gaze flies to Jed and his face turns beet red.

"Is there something we need to know?" Adam asks, patting Jed on the back.

"Rylan's about to score." Jed points at the field.

"He's a good player," the woman says to Ethel.

I look back at her now that they've scored. She has the same crystal-blue eyes as Logan. If his mom is here, that means he must be as well. But where?

"Excuse me," I say to the woman.

She looks at me, blinks, and shakes her head. "Nikki!" she shouts so loudly, I think everyone in the arena heard her. "I didn't see you sneak in." She comes down the bleachers and slides between Molly and me.

"Let me get out of your way," Molly says, standing and heading toward the other side of the bleachers.

I have no time to process where Molly's going because Logan's mom's arms are around me, swaying us back and forth.

"It's so great to meet you. Gosh, you're beautiful, no wonder my son is so smitten." She draws back, leaving her hands on my upper arms, her gaze skating up and down my body. "You're stunning."

I feel my cheeks heat. "Thank you. He has your eyes."

She nods. "Yeah, they're a curse and a blessing. People love them, but they reveal everything you're thinking."

She's right, because right now all I see is happiness beaming from hers.

"Where is he?" I ask.

I don't want to admit I thought he was running late and probably not coming at all. I mean, he doesn't have to. Rylan might be his brother-in-law right now, but he won't be in three months. Logan needs to concentrate on his fighting more than winning over my family. If they like him, it'll only make our breakup that much worse.

She points across the way and I watch Calista roll her eyes at Rylan while he gets high fives from their teammates. Behind them, on the team bench, is Logan.

"Why is he over there?" I ask.

"Rylan wanted him there," his mom says. "I'm Pauline, by the way."

"It's great to meet you."

She swings her arm around my shoulders. "You're just so cute, and your family is wonderful. Your grandma is a hoot," she whispers.

"Yeah. She's something."

I love Ethel like my own grandmas. One lives in Arizona and we barely speak. My mom's mom lives in Sunrise Bay, but she and my grandpa go on a lot of vacations since they've retired.

"I give her credit, she just got Logan to agree to do a self-defense class at the retirement center." Pauline smiles as if that's the best news.

Cade and Adam laugh.

"Good luck to the poor bastard," Cade says to Adam.

"Hey now. Those are my peeps you're talking about." Ethel smacks Cade on the back of the head.

"I'm way too old for you to be doing that," he says.

"As long as I have two feet above the ground, you're not too old for me to take you over my knee."

Apparently concerned, Cade quiets down.

For the rest of the game, my gaze strays to Logan on the bench. I'm not even sure if he's a soccer fan or not, but he's right there, cheering for the team.

Finally, during the last play, Rylan kicks the ball to Calista. She gets past a defender and kicks it back to Rylan, then somehow the ball ends up back with Calista and she shoots and scores. Her arms raise and she runs toward their coach. He picks her up and swings her around, then the team all give her high fives. Well, everyone but Rylan. Sometimes he's such a sourpuss.

"Well, he's not going to get her with that attitude. Someone give that boy some honey," Pauline says.

Mom stands. "I'd like to take him over my knee."

Mom walks over to the Bailey bleachers and talks to Calista's parents. Her dad owns Terra and Mare, the most expensive restaurant in the area.

"She just doesn't understand twelve-year-old boys." Hank shakes his head and follows Mom over there.

"Give the kid a break. He passed her the ball. That's progress." Jed stomps down the bleachers. "I gotta get back to the brewery."

"Oh, can I catch a ride?" Molly asks, already heading down the bleachers.

My eyebrows scrunch. She said nothing about having to work. Jed looks at Cade and for a moment I think he's going to say no, but he nods.

"I'll catch you later, Nik." Molly pats me on the knee and follows my older brother out the door.

"Are those two a couple?" Pauline asks.

"No," I say.

Cade groans behind me. He better not know something I don't. Molly and Jed are great on their own, but I can't imagine if they got together. What if something happened? Molly comes to all our family events, and if Jed broke her heart, it would put a big strain on that. And right now, I have enough problems.

Logan comes over and sits down on the bleacher next to me. "So you met my mom."

"I did." I smile at Pauline. "I thought maybe you forgot to come."

His smile dims, but he recovers immediately, putting his hand on my knee. God, I love the feeling of the warmth from his palm that seeps through my jeans. "I said I'd come."

I nod. He hasn't disappointed me—yet.

We stand, and Pauline is already talking with my sister Mandi while everyone else disperses.

"Mom, you ready?" Logan asks.

"Actually, Mandi here has graciously given me a room that just opened up at her inn. She said it's closer to town."

"Yeah, but you can stay with us." Logan puts his arm around my waist.

In truth, if his mom stays with us, I might have to stop hiding out in my room at night. I only do it because I'm afraid I'm going to sleep with the man. Every night he asks me if I want to work out with him or watch television and I always say no. The man is temptation incarnate and I only have so much willpower.

"Nonsense, you guys are newlyweds. You need your privacy." She looks at Mandi. "I'll just get my bag and head over there with you?"

"Are you sure?" Logan asks.

"Definitely. We'll have plenty of time to catch up."

"Okay." Logan lets it go.

I should be relieved that she's not staying with us, especially if she believes, like my parents, that this is a real marriage. So why do I feel a little disappointed?

LATER THAT NIGHT, I can't sleep, so I walk downstairs to the kitchen. I find Logan, setting out the sugar and spoon next to my empty coffee mug. I figured it was Iris, his chef, who was doing that.

"You're the one who sets all that out?" I ask, sliding into a chair at the kitchen table.

He looks over his shoulder and the tips of his ears grow red. "Guilty. You always seem to be running late."

I laugh because he's not wrong. Having an early morning show isn't ideal for someone who loves to sleep in. "Thank you."

It's a thoughtful gesture. No one has ever done that for me before.

"You're welcome."

"Why are you up?" I ask.

He grabs a package of Twinkies from the cupboard and puts it in front of me. "I couldn't sleep. You?"

"Same." I've been having a horrible time sleeping since I moved in here and I can't figure out why. The mattress is comfortable. I feel safe. Part of me has contemplated that it could be that Logan sleeps down the hall from me.

He joins me at the table with a Ho Ho in hand.

"Would Craig be okay with you eating that?"

He laughs and puts an entire Ho Ho into his mouth. "No," he mumbles around it.

"You cheat a lot," I say.

He shrugs. "I haven't been able to find my groove yet. Doesn't speak well for my fight." He finishes off the other Ho Ho.

"Why do you think that is?" I take a bite of my Twinkie and bring my leg up so my foot rests on the end of the chair.

"You," he says.

I scoff. "Let's remember whose idea this fake marriage was. I was perfectly happy with a divorce."

He laughs and holds up his hands. "I know, and it's the truth." He pauses. "Can I ask you a question?"

"Sure."

"Do you remember our wedding night at all?"

"I remember the balcony and not much else," I admit, embarrassed.

"Consider yourself lucky."

My foot drops to the floor and I lean over the table. "You remember marrying me?"

He shakes his head. "No."

"Then what do you remember?"

His eyelids droop with desire and he shrugs as if suggesting I know what he remembers.

"Oh..."

"Yeah," he says.

"Us?" I waggle a finger between us like I can't form the word sex. He remembers having sex with me. Damn it, why am I jealous?

He nods.

"Oh… was it, um… good?" I hate not having the same memory he does.

"If it wasn't, would I be here? Would I be struggling with my training?"

"Well, I mean, you've had sex with a lot of people during your life."

His forehead crinkles and I think maybe I offended him.

"I can't be the best." My hand comes up and covers my mouth. What am I saying?

He laughs and moves to stand at the same time I get up to escape this conversation. Our chests brush and I stumble to find my footing, but Logan swings his arm around my waist, catching me.

The laughter dies in his throat and silence falls over the kitchen while he stares into my eyes. "You have no idea the torture you put me through."

"What?" I whisper.

"Every night, all I want to do is walk down the hall into your bedroom and bury myself inside you. I want to feel the softness of your body pressed to mine. I want to kiss every inch of you. I want to taste you and spend the entire night fucking you until the sun comes up, then I want to sleep the day away with you in my arms."

I open my mouth, but nothing comes out.

"Say something?" he mumbles.

"Logan," I sigh because I can't think of anything but him right now.

He rights me so I'm on both feet then releases me, stepping away. "Yeah, that's what I thought. Just forget I said anything."

"Logan," I say after him, but he walks out of the room.

Seconds later, his bedroom door shuts with a click and my heart sinks.

But I'm not sure what he expects. He asked me to agree to this fake arrangement, then he explains how desperately he wants me. I might as well just open up my chest, hand him my heart, and say I'm okay with him returning it in pieces.

Chapter Sixteen

Logan

Craig and I finish a round of sparring and each sit down to drink water. "This past week, you've been on fire. Your jabs and kicks look good," he says, then downs half of his water.

"Thanks."

He doesn't have to know I've been taking all my aggravation with Nikki out on him in the ring. I've added another workout to my day since Nikki doesn't want anything to do with me. Her new routine is she doesn't even come to the house for dinner, saying she's putting together a business plan for her podcast or visiting with one person or another until late.

So I've been keeping my distance. I feel as though I've done so much to try to bridge the gap between us, and I was honest about remembering us having sex that night. But she doesn't care because I'm not the kind of guy she sees herself marrying—regardless of the fact that I *am* the guy she's married. At this point, I'm done.

"Wife not giving it up in bed?" Craig asks jokingly, although he's hit the nail on the head.

"I just finally got my head out of my ass." I finish my water.

Nikki's brother Fisher walks into the gym with a brunette I don't recognize. I've only met the guy one time and that was at Rylan's soccer game. He's the sheriff, so he only stopped by to see if they won, then he got a call he had to go out on.

"Hey." He waves and walks over.

"You're friends with the sheriff?" Craig asks with humor in his tone.

"He's Nikki's brother... er... stepbrother." I'm finally starting to figure out who everyone is.

We shake hands and I introduce him to Craig.

"This is Allie," Fisher says.

I nod. "Nice to meet you."

"So you're really in Sunrise Bay and you're married to Fisher's sister?" Allie asks. "We had bets going at the hospital that someone was making it up."

I laugh. "Here in the flesh." I don't address the marriage part because who knows how much longer that'll be true.

"Yes, you are," Allie says.

Fisher gives her a look I'm way too familiar with. One that suggests he doesn't like the fact she's ogling my body.

"Well, we're gonna work out. If you need me to jump in the ring with you, let me know." Fisher bumps fists with me.

"Sure."

Craig laughs and we watch them walk away. I jump into the ring again.

"I think you've done enough ring work today." Craig hops down.

"Come on. One more round. I need work on my elbow jab." I bounce from foot to foot, waving him into the cage.

He groans but joins me. "That's it after this. You need a break. You've gone from twenty miles to one hundred." He puts his gloves and helmet back on and his mouthpiece in.

"Come on."

He rolls his eyes. "You do know this is why Vince doesn't want you with Nikki, right?" Bouncing from foot to foot, he meets me in the center of the ring.

"Don't say that name," I say.

"Oh fuck me. You and Nikki already on the outs after you moved all the way up here?"

"I meant Vince." I circle him and throw a punch, which he blocks.

"Where is he anyway?" Craig asks. "Usually he's asking me how many times you shit in a day, he wants so many specifics on your training."

Craig is right, and that's been my question as well, which is why I checked out Vince's social media last night. My gut proved right. He's trying to recruit some up-and-coming MMA fighters. A part of me is pissed and another part is relieved. He'd only be a dick to Nikki if he was here.

"He's out and about, looking at some younger guys."

Craig stops and I get in a kick in that takes him to the floor. I hold out my hand to help him back up to his feet. "You're fucking with me, right? You're not about to retire, are you?"

"I don't know. Today, no." My answer is honest.

"I was going to say do not put that out there until you win this fight."

"Why?"

He jabs at me, and I get him around and push my elbow

toward his nose. That's the move I have to perfect if I'm going to beat Rinaldo.

"Because we both know that if you lose—"

I give him a look to tell him to watch his words.

He laughs. "If the unthinkable happens, you won't be retiring."

"Come on, I don't think winning is the only thing that matters."

"Log, we both know you're not the kind of person who retires on the bottom. If you leave this sport, you're gonna do it on top."

Craig knows me well. I can't deny he's telling the truth. It's the reason I'd never announce my retirement now unless something major happened.

The doors to the gym open and I glance over to find Nikki coming in from work. Craig kicks my legs out from under me and I crash to the floor right as she looks over.

Great.

I hop up on my feet. "Oh, look, it's the wife."

Nikki says hi to Fisher then comes over. "Hey."

"Give me a minute," I say to Craig.

"Hey, Nikki. Want my protective gear?" Craig laughs and slides out of the ring. He pulls out his cell phone and heads outside where cell service is better.

"What's up?" I ask her, not getting out of the ring.

"I thought maybe we could talk."

I slide under the ropes and sit on the edge. "Sure."

"Ethel's self-defense thing is tonight, and I want us to be talking before. She'll realize something is up and she'll corner us." She crosses her arms.

I take off my gloves and set them beside me, then work on my ankle braces. "Don't worry about it. I can handle it myself."

She laughs. "You might think you can, but you can't. I promise you, those old folks are hard to corral."

"Aren't half of them in wheelchairs and use canes? I think I can handle myself."

Her shoulders fall. "Fine. Go ahead and deal with it on your own."

She storms off. I watch her back as she swings the door open and flies out of the gym.

Craig returns a minute later. "Wifey doesn't look happy."

"Don't worry about it."

Craig sits on a bench, putting on his sweatshirt and pants. "I know you came from a rough neighborhood, that you and Pauline were poor, but do you ever think that all these years, you're used to getting what you want pretty easily?"

"What are you talking about?"

He quirks an eyebrow, glances at Fisher, and back at me.

"We're married," I say.

"Come on, Log, be straight with me. You and that girl aren't even sleeping in the same bed."

I look over my shoulder, but Fisher's staring pretty intently at Allie doing sit-ups.

"What?" I ask.

"You like her, but whatever you two are right now, it isn't husband and wife."

"You don't know what you're talking about." I shove my stuff in my bag.

"Maybe, but hear me out. Sometimes when you've gotten everything you've ever wanted and worked for in your life, it's hard to fathom how someone could see anything as impossible. But for some people, believing in something can be hard. Give the girl some time to come around."

"I've given her time," I say, basically admitting to what he suspects.

"What? Two weeks?"

I sit and stare down at the floor. Craig has a point. But I feel like I've done everything to prove myself to her, and I've taken her nos to mean that she's not into me.

"Thanks," I say.

He pats my back. "Hey, I gotta keep you in the right frame of mind. I like Nikki, by the way. She's good for you. You don't want one of those women who just fall at your feet. Right?"

He is right. I grab my phone from my bag.

> Sorry. I'd appreciate it if you went with me to the retirement center.

Three dots appear then disappear before her message flashes up on the screen.

> Okay. I'll drive. Let's leave at six.

> Sounds good.

Although I don't want her to drive, right now is probably not the time to make an argument out of it.

"I'm proud of you. It takes a real man to know when he's wrong." Craig clasps me on the shoulder and laughs.

We walk out of Pump It Up. "Who the hell told you that? A woman, I assume?"

"Yep, and it's the best advice I've ever gotten."

We walk toward the house and I recommit to giving Nikki her space, even if I want to go to battle with her over her fear of letting someone in.

Chapter Seventeen

Nikki

Six o'clock rolls around and Logan comes downstairs from his bedroom, freshly showered and smelling amazing.

"Hey, I thought I'd be ready before you." He stops at the front table and puts his wallet and keys into his pocket.

I turn on my heel to head toward the door. "You look too good to go to a retirement center. Especially since you're teaching self-defense."

He makes me look shameful in my leggings and sweatshirt. Grandma Ethel will surely have something to say about my attire in front of her friends.

"I'm wearing workout clothes." He looks down at himself as if he forgot what he was wearing.

"Yes, but your hair is styled and you smell good."

He smirks. "So what you're really saying is that you think I'm hot?" Before I can manage a rebuttal, he puts up his finger. "And that I smell good."

I roll my eyes playfully because he caught me. "Let's go." I open the front door and we step off the porch.

"I can drive us," he says, pulling out his keys.

"I said I'd drive." I unlock my car.

"Well, I'd like to drive. I need to try to figure out where things are, and I haven't ventured into Lake Starlight yet." He presses on his key fob and the taillights of the truck he's renting flash.

I lock my car. "Fine, but I know what you're doing."

He opens the passenger door for me. "And that would be?"

"You think you're the man, so you have to drive. Like if I drive you, that somehow makes you less manly." I slide into his truck and put on my seat belt. He stands outside and doesn't close the door.

"You're right." He shuts the door and rounds the back of the truck.

My jaw is still hanging open when he slides into his seat. "You actually admit it?"

He turns the key in the ignition while his gaze remains on me. "I know it might be chauvinistic, but it's just my belief. It doesn't mean I think I'm the better driver. I just feel like it's my job as your husband to drive you."

"You don't believe women are bad drivers?" That would be a deal breaker.

He laughs and puts the truck in gear. "No. Not at all."

I blow out a breath and ignore the small part of me that likes him wanting to drive me around. Ever since I can remember, I've taken care of myself. My mom is great and did more than what she needed to when I was growing up, but since moving out of her house, I've taken things on myself. I'm not like my sisters or stepsisters, who usually call one of our brothers when we need something heavy lifted or need something hung at the house. It's nice to have someone take care of me for once, even if it is just driving.

"So do you have a game plan?" I ask as we leave Sunrise Bay and head toward Lake Starlight.

He laughs. "I looked up some stuff and Craig gave me some tips. But I'm gonna be honest, I can't very well flip one of them over my shoulder to demonstrate. I'm not sure I'm equipped to do this class."

I bite my lip. How the hell does anyone teach a bunch of elderly people self-defense? "Surely you have something like pinch this and that and the person will go down."

He glances at me. "Ethel and Dori could probably beat the shit out of me in a dark alley."

"Only because you wouldn't fight back."

He shrugs. "True, but the two of them together are scary. They'd scare any criminal."

I laugh because he's right. There are times I want to scream at Ethel to stop talking about her late husband and the sex they had. She's very open, which is great, but I don't want to picture it.

"Probably. Take a right here, then you'll see the entrance." I touch his thigh without thinking. His strong leg muscle flexes and I think better of it and remove my hand. "Thank you for doing this, by the way."

"It's not a problem. Ethel and Dori have been nothing but nice to me since I got here."

A mile down the road, he turns into the long driveway of Northern Lights Retirement Center.

He parks the truck as I glance at the building. "I'll just apologize now for whatever happens in there."

He turns off the ignition and slides out of the truck. I open my door and join him where he was coming to let me out. "What can really go wrong?"

I raise my eyebrows at him and shake my head. "Remember that when we're leaving and you're so distraught, I'm the one driving home."

He swings his arm around my shoulders to pull me closer. "Never gonna happen."

Oh, how innocent he is now.

We walk into the lobby and I can already hear someone bossing someone else around in the main room.

The program director, Leann, approaches us. "When your grandma told me about this, I was skeptical, but..." Her gaze greedily swallows up Logan. "I think it will be good for them and they'll trust someone like you. They've spent the afternoon watching your last fight."

Could she at least *try* to hide her attraction to Logan? I remind myself I have nothing to be jealous of—I'm not even invested in this marriage. But Leann doesn't know that.

"That was amazing when you got him pinned," she says.

Logan smiles. "Good to know someone thinks I'm talented. This one sat there filing her nails." Logan points his thumb at me.

"Oh, we saw a glimpse of you and Molly. I have no idea how you just sat there uninterested," Leann says.

"It's not really my thing." I hook my arm through Logan's because he may not really be my man, but hell if I'm gonna stand here while some woman who thinks he is flirts with him.

He glances at my arm and smirks. "She's lying. It turns her on. She was all over me that night."

I stare at him with my most bored expression. Although he has a memory of that portion of the night and I don't, I'm embarrassed just thinking about how I might've been when we had sex.

Leann is quiet for a moment, then she smiles at me. "Anyway, let's get you in there."

We follow her to the room for big events. There's a mat on the ground in front of the residents. Some are in wheelchairs and others are sitting in chairs with canes hanging off the back of them.

"Shh, everyone, my granddaughter is here." Ethel stands and walks over to us. "And her husband, Logan Stone."

The room cheers for Logan but not for me. Whatever. Let's see what they think of him after he breaks someone's hip.

Logan waves as if he just entered the ring and I say hello.

"I'm so excited. Leann put out the mats. Do you want me to go first?" Ethel asks.

Logan looks at me. "How about I just use Nikki to demonstrate?"

"What?" My mouth drops open. I thought I'd be a spectator.

Ethel looks me up and down. "Isn't that why you're dressed like that?"

I shake my head. "Why would I need to dress up to come here?"

Ethel touches my neckline. "A necklace would have at least made you look a little nicer."

"A necklace with my yoga pants and sweatshirt? I'll remember that next time." I look at her. "What about your leisure suit?"

She straightens the elastic waistband of the zip-up pink jacket that matches her pants. "I match. And my hair is done."

"So is mine."

She touches my ponytail. "It's pulled up."

I glance at Logan. "Let's get this show on the road." I

strip off my sweatshirt and drop it on a table, then I walk to the mat and take off my shoes. "Flip me around," I tell Logan.

"That's what she said," a man says, and everyone laughs.

Ethel goes back and sits down. I love the woman, but sometimes I understand the phrase "drive you to drink."

"What does your T-shirt say?" Midge, who Ethel's brought around a few times, lowers her glasses and leans forward.

I straighten my shirt. "It says, 'Don't mind me, I'm here for the tea.'"

"You drink tea?" Midge asks. "Which kind? I only drink herbal. Once my daughter-in-law sent me this tea box with all these flavors, and I had one before bed. I was up all night."

"Oh no, tea means gossip."

Midge's forehead crinkles and she pushes up her black-rimmed glasses.

"What did she say?" the old man to her right says. "I was distracted while I was reading her shirt."

My head swivels to Logan and he bites his lip from laughing so hard.

"Shouldn't my husband stick up for me?" I whisper, although I'm not sure I had to for them not to hear me.

"She said she likes tea and gossip," Midge says.

"No. Tea means gossip," I correct, but Midge doesn't hear me.

Logan places his hand on my bicep and pulls me back. "You can't blame the man."

Logan ogles my chest, and I narrow my eyes. He laughs and tears off his sweatshirt. His T-shirt is one of his own—Logan "The Pit Bull" Stone. It's faded as if he's worn it a million times and, damn, he looks sexy in it.

"Okay, ladies and gentlemen. I'm Logan Stone." He gives a small wave. "I'm a professional MMA fighter."

"We saw you earlier. Enjoy those women with the signs now because your body doesn't stay fit forever," the man who was talking to Midge says.

Midge smacks him over the head. "He's a married man."

"Married to who?" the man asks.

"Nikki. Ethel's granddaughter." She points at me.

"The one who drinks tea?" he asks, and I sigh, my head falling back.

"Tea means…" I wave it off. "Forget it."

"Isaac and Midge, be quiet and let the poor man show you how to defend yourself," Leann, the activities director, scolds them.

Isaac stands with the aid of his cane. "You want to know how I defend myself?" He pulls out the top of his cane to show a knife. A sizable one that looks shiny and sharp.

Logan instinctively moves back and throws an arm around my waist like a mom does in a car when she brakes too fast.

"We're not young like you." The man looks to a few men for confirmation and they all nod, holding up their canes.

I better warn Ethel and Dori to cool it with the sarcasm around here.

"Oh boy, I'm not sure you're allowed to have those in here." Leann steps forward.

Isaac puts the knife back, holding the cane to his body.

"This is what I do." A woman digs her hand into her bra, revealing a can of mace. She holds it out in front of her with her finger on the nozzle.

"Oh, that's great," I say, inching forward to get her finger off the canister, but she presses it.

Logan tackles me to the floor, covering his body with mine.

"OOOUUCCCHHHH!" the woman screams, and Leann rushes over.

I glimpse over Logan's shoulder and see the poor woman has sprayed herself in the eyes.

"I'll be back. Come on, Olive, we'll get the eye cleaner, and I'll call 911." Leann leaves us.

Logan's still on top of me. The weight of his body feels too nice. Our eyes lock and heat funnels straight between my thighs.

"Thank you," I say a little breathlessly.

"I think she likes more than tea," Isaac says.

Logan laughs, rises flawlessly from the floor, and offers me his hand. Man, he makes it hard not to sleep with him.

"Flip her on her back again," a woman who I think is Dori yells.

"Ready?" Logan asks, getting into position. "I won't hurt you."

"Okay."

He grabs my arm, tugging me into his body, then he swipes my legs out from under me. This time he's got me on my stomach with my arms spread above my head.

"I like that position. What's it called? Doggie-style, right?" Isaac asks.

"Such dirty minds," Midge says with disapproval in her tone.

"That's not what you said last night," he says, and Midge's glasses fog up.

Logan helps me back up and I raise my eyebrows.

"Was I right?" I whisper.

He laughs again. "This is the most fun I've had since I got here."

I tilt my head. "Why's that?"

"Because I get to fling you around. There's only one bad part."

"Do I even want to know?"

"We're fully clothed."

I'm certain there's no hiding my flushed face.

Damn it if I don't feel exactly the same. And that's a problem.

Logan

The minute I tell Nikki it's the best night of my visit, she shuts down. I show a few moves to the seniors, but in truth, they're probably better with their knives and mace. One woman said she carries a stun gun. By the time we're all served ice cream as if this is a Boy Scout meeting, a small part of me thinks I should put up a sign in the community to warn would-be criminals about them.

We're seated around a few tables, and I'm with the guy named Isaac and another guy named Earl. All they seem to care about is whether the boobs on the women who hold up the signs in the ring are real.

"I honestly don't know," I answer again, my gaze straying over to Nikki, who's still trying to explain to Midge that tea isn't actual tea. She should give up that fight now.

Earl leans in. "Come on. We won't tell Nikki or Ethel. Look at you, you're telling me you've never had sex with one of them?" He looks at Isaac. "I don't believe this guy."

I shake my head, scooping my chocolate ice cream out of the dish. I'm not getting into it with these two. "How about we change topics?"

"Okay, how many women do you get on a weekly basis?" Isaac asks. "Do you believe in reincarnation? Because I'd like to come back as you."

I laugh and finish off my ice cream, leaning back in the chair. "I'm a married man." I hold up my hand, showing off the ring I bought for myself so we can continue this charade.

So many times, I've wanted to tell Nikki the truth that I couldn't care less about our deal and I'm here to see where this goes. But she's made it clear that she can't handle, or doesn't want to handle, anything to do with her heart.

When I pinned her, I felt her rapid heartbeat and the way she sighed when my weight was over her. The slight movement she made underneath me like maybe it wouldn't be the worst thing if we did this when we weren't in front of a group of elderly people watching our every move. I want to confront her, but she's still far from ready. Every time I think we've made progress, she retreats.

"Fine, you can come back by yourself some other day and tell us the real story." Isaac winks.

I laugh. "I'm serious. I'm not the type to sleep around."

Isaac winks again. "Sure, you aren't."

"I hope you're telling the truth because if I were you, I wouldn't want Ethel or Dori on my back for anything I did. They're scary, especially as a team." Earl scoops his ice cream, looking at the women in question.

Isaac waves. "Don't listen to him, he likes Dori. If he could stay awake long enough, maybe they could get it on." Isaac laughs at his own joke.

"I have narcolepsy, okay? It's beyond my control."

Isaac rolls his eyes. "Whatever."

"Midge is blind once you take her glasses off and that's the only reason she sleeps with you," Earl hammers back.

I stand to excuse myself before I have any more visuals thrust into my head that will keep me up tonight. "It's been a pleasure, guys. I'm sure I'll be back."

"I'm sure you will. Ethel's always swindling her grandkids to come in and do something with us," Earl says and waves.

Isaac crooks his finger for me to get closer. "Get me some pictures next time and I'll pay you ten dollars."

I pat him on the shoulder. "You're a funny man, Isaac."

I disregard his question and leave to go join my wife. Taking a chair, I turn it around and straddle it next to Nikki. She glances at me, smiles, and looks at her table.

"Are you ready to go?" she asks.

"No rush. Whenever."

She finishes her ice cream quickly as though she wants to go. "Thanks, Grandma and Dori. Hope you enjoyed Logan."

"Not as much as you're going to." Midge lowers her glasses and checks me out. "I wish I had a quarter to bounce off that butt."

"Midge!" Nikki squeaks and her eyes widen.

"I might be old and wrinkly, but I'm still a woman." She pushes her glasses back up.

I smile tentatively.

"You've scared the poor boy," Dori says. "Go, you two. Have fun at home. Be watchful of Sheriff Miller, no erratic driving." She waves her finger.

Nikki pushes at my side. "We need to go."

"Bye, everyone." I wave and they all wave back, saying their goodbyes.

Once we're outside, Nikki stops touching me, as though we're strangers again, and my body runs cold.

"They're good people, just a little odd, that's all." I open the door of the truck and she climbs in.

"Thanks again," she says, and I shut the door, rounding the truck.

My annoyance is getting the better of me. I really don't want to have an outburst with her, but I'm done with this standoffish side of her every time we grow closer.

I pull out of the parking lot, out to the main road of Lake Starlight. We pass the infamous resort, Glacier Point, the small-town shops, then we're on the highway back to Sunrise Bay. Lake Starlight is nice and maybe I'm not impartial, but I like that Sunrise Bay doesn't have parking in the square, you have to park outside of it. It's safer for the kids and families.

Jesus, when did I start thinking about the safety of children and prefer one small town over another? What's happened to me in the short time I've lived here?

The twenty-minute ride is quiet. Nikki sits without saying much. By the time we pull up to my rented house, she's ready to bolt. When the car door shuts behind her and I watch her walk up to the house, the last ounce of my patience snaps.

I turn off the ignition and slam the truck door, following her up the walkway. She uses her key to get in and is on the bottom stair to head upstairs when I make it through the door.

"Going to hide out in your room for the rest of the night?" I head toward the kitchen without waiting for an answer.

"What's that supposed to mean?" she asks, never stepping down from the stair.

"Nothing," I mumble and continue down the hallway. Yeah, I'm being passive-aggressive, but I'm not sure what to do at this point.

"It doesn't sound like nothing," she says, her footsteps sounding behind me.

"I guess you had to be around me for an unbearable amount of time and now you're going to hibernate in your room for the rest of the evening." I open the fridge, still hungry, and pull out one of my juices.

"Is that going to fill you up?" She eyes my juice.

I gulp down another swallow. "What do you care?"

She leans her hip against the counter. "Tell me again what's wrong with you."

I lower the juice and set it on the counter, then stare at her for a moment. Do I really want to do this now? Call her out? Hell yeah, I do. Even if it ends with me leaving town and heading back to Vegas. I can't stand it anymore. I never would have thought she'd be this hard to crack.

"The fact that you won't even allow me to get close to you. You act like I'm some diseased animal."

She scoffs. "A little dramatic, don't you think?"

I shake my head. "No, I don't think I'm being dramatic. I think you act dramatic when you try to ignore the fact that you have feelings."

She scoffs again and crosses her arms. All I see is her chest in that T-shirt. "What feelings? Feelings for you?" Her tone suggests it's a ludicrous accusation.

"Yes. Feelings. For me. You're trying to hide them. Or ignore them."

"I told you—"

I hold up my hand before she can finish. "Yeah, daddy issues. Got it." I walk away, but as I'm escaping the room, she stops me.

"You have no idea how messed up I am over it. And the fact that you're... well... you, doesn't help."

I twirl around. "The fact I'm me? Did I invite some girl home with me? Have I given anyone any suggestion that I'm single while I've been here? I uprooted my entire life to be here with you."

She laughs—an ungenuine one at that. "I never asked you to. *You* asked *me* to pretend the marriage was real until after your fight."

I place my hands on my hips and my chin drops in defeat. She has a point. I did do that. "I only did that because I wanted to see where this goes. I felt something in my gut that told me there's a reason we got married, something special between us. But you pushed me away, and I felt like the only way to explore it was to make that deal."

"What?" she whispers. "You fooled me?"

I shake my head. "I was giving you the five contacts no matter what. I did it to buy time. Time with you. Time to explore this, but all I get from you is the palm of your hand in the air."

"Yeah, because I felt like you wanted me to play the role, but didn't really want me," she says.

"You really believed that?" I ask. Is she really that bad at reading signs? "You said you didn't play games."

"And so did you. But you just played me." She clenches her fists at her sides. "You tricked me, and now you're angry that I'm not stripping down naked every night and sliding into bed with you."

I throw my hands in the air. "I'm mad because you're ignoring the pull we have toward one another. I see you looking at me, Nikki. I see your cheeks flush when I get near. I felt your heartbeat when I was on top of you tonight, the slight shift in your hips. Admit it to yourself at least, if you won't to me. You want me just as much as I want you."

She blows out a breath. "You don't even remember marrying me."

"Yet here I am!" I open my arms wide for her. "Waiting for you to want anything to do with me. Waiting for you to admit that there's something here that neither of us can put into words and that it's good, with the potential to be really fucking great."

She shakes her head and fear flashes in her eyes. "You probably say that to all kinds of women."

"For the love of—" I inhale a deep breath and force myself to calm down. "I'm not a womanizer. I don't make a habit of marrying women in Vegas and following them to their hometown. You're the only woman I've ever done that for."

"How do I believe you, when I don't know you?" she asks in a quiet voice.

I step forward. "Because you trust me until I give you reason not to."

She looks up, and I take another step forward. Her eyes plead with me to make her cross over her bridge of doubt. In her eyes, I see a scared woman who's afraid of what will happen if she takes a risk. But I can't be the one to force her. She has to want to do it for herself.

"I'm not sure I can."

"Why not?" I'm chest to chest with her, my hands begging to touch her. "I won't hurt you."

Her eyes meet mine. "And I'm sure that's what my dad told my mom once upon a time. But he didn't have to see the look on her face when I told her he was with another woman. I'll never forget that face." Tears well in her eyes and she places her hand on my heart. "I'm sorry, Logan, I just can't."

She walks around me, down the hall, up the stairs, and a second later, her bedroom door quietly shuts.

I blow out a breath. All I can say is I tried. Tomorrow I'll tell Craig and the team that we're headed back to Vegas. I'm not gonna find what I came here looking for. I need to put my time in Sunrise Bay aside.

Chapter Nineteen

Nikki

I sit on the bed and stare at the wall. The image of Logan's blue eyes, which usually sparkle with genuine kindness, falling into despair after I told him I couldn't step forward and meet him halfway is burned into my brain. I toe out of my shoes, annoyed that my dad is ruining this for me because of my trust issues.

I pick up the phone and call Molly. She answers on the first ring.

"Hey, girl." From the sounds of it, she's still at the brewery.

"Busy?" I ask, shrugging out of my yoga pants and panties, replacing them with my pajama set bottoms.

"For you, never."

"No need for work to interfere," Cade says in the background.

"Don't worry, I flipped him off for you." She laughs. "I'm going to take this in the office."

Molly's complete disregard for my brothers being her

bosses pulls a smile out of me. I hear a door close, and the sounds of glasses clinking and people's laughter in the background disappears.

"So what's wrong?" she asks.

"Why do you assume something is wrong?" I put her on speaker and tear off my shirt before putting on my pajama shirt and buttoning it up the front. After a good night's sleep, I'll be able to regroup with Logan.

"You have that sound in your voice."

"What sound?"

"Just tell me. I've been your best friend for way too long not to know when something is going on."

I roll over on my back and take the phone off speaker in case Logan comes upstairs. "Why am I so messed up?"

She laughs.

"I'm serious, Mol, what is wrong with me? Relationships terrify me."

"I assume this is about Logan?"

"No, it's about the mailman. Yes, of course, it's about Logan."

"If you're gonna be snippy, I'm not gonna help you."

She'll always help me. We both know that, but I'm not going to call her on it right now, just in case.

"He wants to pursue this. He told me that the whole reason..." I forgot that I never told Molly about the arrangement we made. It's been our secret. I know I can trust Molly, but I never wanted to chance the truth coming out for Logan's sake.

"Whole reason what?"

I sigh. "When Logan first came to town, he said he wanted to pretend that we were happy until the fight was over. That he didn't want the bad press distracting him. In exchange, he's giving me contact with five celebrities to interview on the podcast."

"Interesting," she says.

"What?"

"You honestly believed him when he told you that?" She laughs.

"Why would I not?"

"I know your dad did a number on you. I understand that. Everyone does. Plus, the way he never comes up here to see you guys and stuff. But you're being blind to what's going on. Look at your wedding picture, Nik. Or how about the way Logan's eyes always follow you through a room. Or how it looks like he hangs on every word you say. That whole deal you two made was bullshit."

I sigh and throw my arm over my eyes. "That's what he told me tonight. That he came here because his gut told him he should be here."

"Aw, I really like the guy."

"You liked him before I married him," I say dryly.

"Technically, I liked the way he fought, not actually *him*." She covers up the receiver. "It's Nikki."

"Is that Cade again?" I ask.

"Jed."

"I'll let you go. I don't want him to—" I hear them wrestling over the phone.

"Sorry!" Molly screams in the background which means...

"Nik, get your head out of your ass. Our dad's an asshole, so what? I'm a decent guy," Jed says.

"That's the argument you're going with?" Molly says behind him.

"I am a good guy."

"Um... you're a great flirt," Molly says. "Give me the phone. I'm the one who can talk sense into her."

"No way. I'm her brother, we share the same dipshit father."

They continue having their own conversation.

"I'm gonna go, you guys," I say.

"Give the guy a chance," Jed says. "Hell, give *any* guy a chance to prove you wrong. If Logan's that bad of a guy, I'll be here for you and I promise to pick you up and dust you off."

"You should be offering to kick his ass if he breaks her heart," Molly says.

"Have you seen the guy?" Jed asks incredulously.

"I'm fine, honestly. I just have to think this through."

"Get out of your damn head and do what you want, regardless of the repercussions," my brother says, then I hear them wrestling with the phone again.

"Hey, he's gone now. Just look at your wedding photos, Nik. It's all there." Molly's voice is genuine and heartfelt.

"Thanks."

"Break's over, Molly, get your ass out there." Cade's booming voice chimes in behind her.

"He must've gotten into a fight with Presley because he's in a bad mood tonight. Gotta go. Call me if you need me again."

I laugh. "I'll be fine."

"Just look, Nikki. I know it's scary but have faith."

We say goodbye and I lie there staring at the ceiling, knowing Logan is probably right down the hall in his bedroom by now. He could be doing the same thing I am.

My hands shake as I bring up my phone and type "Logan Stone marriage photos" into my browser. There's my drunken face front and center. I click on the link for some gossip blog and refrain from reading the article, zooming in on the picture like Molly said to do.

I stare at Logan's face and try to look at him as someone on the outside might. We're both looking at each other. I have a bouquet of fake flowers, and Elvis and his wife have just thrown birdseed that's sprinkling down on us. Logan and I are laughing at one another, but it's the look on our faces, like we've known each other forever, that gets me. It's as though there's an inside joke only we share.

I scroll down on the page. There's another picture of us where Logan has me pressed against the open door of the SUV, our lips on one another's. My hand is fisted in his shirt as if I'm afraid he'll get away. The next picture is me crawling in the car and Logan entering right after me. The last picture is of the SUV driving away.

There are so many reasons why I look carefree—tequila likely the biggest—but I don't get that comfortable with men usually. And never in only one night. Maybe I do need to explore this thing between us.

I leave my phone on the bed and sit up, gaining the fortitude to make the move I should've earlier. Rising from the bed, I stare at the door as if it's a wormhole portal that'll take me to another dimension. Do I have the guts to see what's on the other side?

Before I second-guess myself, I walk over and open the door, then I tiptoe down the hall. I knock softly on the door of Logan's bedroom, but there's no answer.

I have a devil on one shoulder and an angel on the other, at odds over what to do. Go back to my room and forget this whole thing or take a chance and hope it ends up okay?

The doorknob twists in my hand and the hinges squeak as I inch the door open, finding an empty bed. That's when I hear water running.

This is my chance. He never has to know I was here. Go back now before I get hurt.

I shake off the negative thoughts and think about the look on Logan's face coming out of the chapel. He's right. There is something between us and I've denied the pull too long.

I walk through the bedroom to the giant master bath with a soaking tub, two-person shower, and two vanity sinks. This is probably where Logan hoped we'd stay together, but I accepted his offer for the other bedroom.

The glass shower door is steamed over, so I can't see him. My hand shakes as I wrap my fingers around the metal handle to pull the door open. I close my eyes and inhale a deep breath before slowly inching it open.

Logan startles then stares at me. He doesn't have to ask me what I'm doing there. Our gazes lock and I step into the shower, joining him.

"Please... just don't hurt me," I whisper.

His arm wraps around my waist and he pulls me to him, under the stream of water, soaking my pajamas so they stick to me like a second skin. "I'll protect your heart with my life."

He bends down and presses the gentlest kiss to my mouth. I savor the softness of his lips compared to the rest of his hard body pressed to mine. My arms wind around his neck, all my worries fading when his tongue slides into my mouth.

I'm so upset that I don't remember the first kiss we ever shared, but if it was as good as this one, then I know why I said, "I do."

Urging me backward until my back hits the wet tiled wall, he breaks our kiss to stare at me. "Does this mean?"

I nod, answering his vague question. "I'm in."

My favorite smile of his, the shy one, emerges and my heart flips and flops inside my chest with happiness.

"About damn time," he mumbles, and his finger and thumb undo one of the buttons on my silk pajamas. He groans at seeing the crevice between my breasts.

Another button comes undone. I watch his masterful fingers unclothe me, finally pulling the wet fabric from my skin and leaving me bare from the waist up. His right hand molds to my breast and his lips descend on mine again, his tongue sliding against mine instantly. I knew he'd be a great kisser. Patient but persistent at the same time. His hard length rubs against my stomach, and I take him in my palm.

"God, you feel good," he says, bucking slowly into my hand while I pump him up and down.

Our tongues fight for dominance. His hand squeezes my breast, his thumb running over my already pebbled nipple. I want him so badly, I find it hard to control myself. My leg wants to rise over his hip so he can slide himself between my legs.

As if he can read my mind, he stops kissing me and sinks to his knees on the shower floor, simultaneously pulling my pajama shorts down my legs. I fight the embarrassment of being completely naked in front of him as he looks up at me with devilish eyes. His hands slowly urge my legs apart and he swings one over his shoulder, his finger running along the length of my core.

My hands fall to his hair, my fingers threading through his blond strands. He replaces his finger with his tongue, licking his way up to my clit before toying with it with the tip of his tongue.

My head falls back to the tile. I have no words to describe how good his mouth feels on me. Why did I wait this long? He's masterful in his movements, shifting from gentle to building more pressure over and over again. His tongue and fingers move in tandem until my orgasm sits right on the precipice. I'm so close, and I'm sure my sighs and panted praises clue him in that I'm about to come.

He doesn't hold back. If anything, he stretches the rubber band further until I can't hold back any longer. My body jolts when I come, tipping forward away from the tile wall, and every muscle fiber in my body tenses before they go limp.

"Holy shit," I murmur.

Logan smiles at me from between my legs and I take a mental snapshot of this moment, determined to remember it always.

His shoulder digs into my stomach as he throws me over his shoulder. "I'm not even close to being done with you yet." He turns off the water then steps out of the shower and walks us into his bedroom, where he deposits me on the bed.

"We'll get it all wet," I say.

"Exactly." He winks and climbs on me, situating his hard length between my legs.

My body buzzes with anticipation, and I push away all my worries and fears so I can enjoy a night I'll never forget. Not this time.

Chapter Twenty

Logan

I really hope I didn't fall in the shower, hit my head, and this is all a dream. Crawling up the bed, careful not to put all my weight on Nikki, this feels like a dream come true. Especially since I've had to relive the memory of having her pressed to the glass in the hotel suite.

She winds her arms around my neck, her fingers fiddling with my wet hair, bringing me down so our lips meet. Her body is so soft and silky, it's a struggle not to just slip inside her.

"Let me get a condom," I murmur, breaking off the kiss, not wanting to get off her.

I reach into the nightstand where I put them since I've hoped she'd come into my bedroom at some point.

"Just so you know, I bought this box for us." I grab the foil packet and rip it open.

She smiles and gets up on her knees and helps me roll it down my length. Talk about a sex goddess. Now she's staring at me with those hooded eyes.

Our bodies collide and I run my hands down her spine to her ass, grabbing a handful in each hand. She yelps and her lips find mine, her tongue sliding into my mouth. I love the fact she can be domineering and bashful at the same time. When I stripped her down naked, a pink flush rushed through her body.

Easing her down on her back, I push up one thigh so her leg is bent, making room for my hips between her legs. She never takes her eyes off me as I push into her, inch by inch, and I'm rewarded with her nails digging into my shoulder blades.

"Are you okay?" I ask before I push in the final couple inches.

"Never better. Keep going."

Once I'm fully encased inside her, I wait a second before I move so that I don't embarrass myself and come in two seconds flat. I think about the tape I watched of Brett Rinaldo the other day, his footwork and his grappling skills. But Nikki's soft pleas pull my attention back to her. I need to find the strength of my willpower right now.

I ease out of her and slide back in, circling my hips, and based on the fact that her eyes fall back in her head, she enjoys it. My gaze stays fixed on her, watching her reactions and her enjoyment as I thrust in and out, doing more of what I can see she loves.

She's so beautiful underneath me. Her pink lips and rosy cheeks. Her eyes are what really drive me insane. She has no idea the amount of truth that projects from them, just like mine. Or maybe she masks it with some people. Right now, she's scared but taking a chance on me and there's no way I'm going to fuck this up.

"Please, Logan, don't stop," she says, panting for a breath.

I lower myself to my elbows on either side of her head. I kiss her, and soon we find a rhythm as though this isn't our first time. It isn't, but we were both too drunk to fully remember the events of that night. She praises my skills and I tell her how beautiful she is. Her hands run up and down my back then cling to my shoulders when I take small breaks to suck on her nipples.

By the time my orgasm hits, I shift her one leg up on my shoulder, driving deeper inside, and she combusts, her walls clenching around my dick. That's endgame for me. I pump into her two more times before I still inside her, seeing total blackness for a moment as I spill inside the condom.

My eyes adjust and I lower my body, sliding out of her, and fall to my back, catching my breath for a moment. She shifts beside me and I worry that she's going to get up and leave. Maybe this was all about sexual tension for her, and now that she's had her release, she's done. But I'm pleasantly surprised when she kisses me and says she'll be right back. She walks into the bathroom, and I hear the toilet flush and the sink faucet turn on. I'm hyperaware of her movements when I should be enjoying that she's giving me a shot.

Walking out of the master bathroom, she slides under the sheets. I excuse myself to get rid of the condom. On the way back, I grab the remote by the television.

"Are you hungry?" I ask.

She shakes her head, so I slide into the bed with her. She cuddles up to me, her wet hair on my shoulder, her soft body pressed to mine. Damn, this feels good.

"How about a movie then?"

She kisses my pec. "Perfect."

I turn on some romantic comedy I assume she'll enjoy and run my hand down her back, loving the feel of her soft tits pressed against my rib cage. A man could get used to this.

––––––––––

THE NEXT MORNING, my alarm goes off and I slam my hand on my phone to get it to stop. Nikki stirs in my arms, and I kiss her temple.

"Go back to sleep," I whisper and slide out of bed.

I don't have a lot of expectations for today's workout. My body is sore from the workout Nikki gave me last night. The movie only lasted fifteen minutes before she was kissing my chest and one thing turned into another. We ended up back in the shower, then went down for a snack at two in the morning. I'm not sure how much sex we had the night of our wedding, but last night, I'm fairly sure we exceeded that.

I'd be lying if I said I wasn't worried about where her head will be with the sunrise, but I'm hoping it remains where it was last night and she's finally crossed over that bridge of doubt.

After pulling on my track pants, a T-shirt, and a sweat-shirt, I brush my teeth and grab my gym shoes, then quietly walk out of the bedroom. I should be home before she even wakes up.

Craig is already stretching outside when I open the front door.

"You're late," he says.

"Like, two minutes." I sit on the porch stairs and put on my shoes.

"You're never late." He gives me a look that makes me think he somehow knows Nikki's in my bed. Which makes no sense because he's the one who doubted our marriage was real. "Wife keeping you up?"

I shake my head, finish tying my gym shoes, and jog in place. "This isn't yoga, let's go."

"You're going to be the one with a Charlie horse." He laughs, and we start on the trail he's mapped out for us. "So..." He elbows me.

I glance over. "What?"

"I don't want details, but last night I woke up in the middle of the night and your kitchen light was on. I saw two shadows."

"You fucking Peeping Tom," I say, and he laughs.

"I wasn't peeking in. I just happened to see. When I saw someone crouch down and then the other's head tilt back, I had the decency to go back to bed."

"How considerate of you," I say dryly.

There's no way I can hide the smile that breaks free from just the memory of having Nikki to myself last night.

Craig pushes me in the shoulder, and I lose my footing for a moment. "You son of a bitch. You took my advice, and it worked."

"Technically no. I tried the whole let it go thing, but after the retirement center, we ended up in a fight." Maybe I should've given her more space, but I feel like I did the right thing.

"I love that. When you're all heated and angry and you just go after one another." Craig jogs to the right up a trail we haven't been on before.

"It didn't happen quite like that. Where the hell are we going?"

"I took this trail the other day and it adds another mile, which you need now that we're getting closer to the fight." He pats my stomach and sprints ahead of me.

"I want to take her on a date," I say. "But I have no idea what we could even do around here."

"I'm sure she's done everything this place has to offer."

I nod. "Exactly. And I don't want it to be cliché."

"You need to fly her out of here then. Go somewhere just the two of you. Without Vince finding out. He keeps calling and asking what the situation is up here."

I shake my head. "If he's so concerned, then why doesn't he just come up here and see for himself what's going on?"

He slows to a steady jog when we hit downtown. "I gotta ask you a question and I want you to be upfront with me." The good humor from earlier is gone.

I slow my pace, wondering what's concerning Craig. "What's up?"

He glances over then away before looking me in the eye. "I know we touched on this before but do you think Rinaldo is your last fight? Are you retiring?"

I stop and throw my head back to catch my breath. Walking, I debate my answer, but I owe Craig the truth. "I'm not sure. I'm getting older, man. Every injury is harder to recover from. I'm sick of the strict diet and training regimen. I want to live a normal life, but at the same time, what the fuck will I do if I retire?"

"I'm pretty sure you don't even have to work."

Craig's right. If I lived a normal life, I'd be good to go with the money I have in the bank, but that's not what I meant.

"Fighting is everything to me. I've always been a fighter. I can't imagine it not being a part of my life."

"Then why are you considering retirement?"

Truth is, besides everything else, I also want a wife and a family. I want to settle down. I'm just not sure now is the right time. "Because I can't do it forever and there are other things I want out of life too. Maybe it's time to start down a different path. Maybe that's what this situation with Nikki is all about. Besides, like I said before—no one wants to go out while they're not on top."

"You're still on top." Craig begins our run again as we head back toward the house.

"Right now."

"And Nikki? What does she think of this?"

I glance at him from the side of my eye. "I've never talked to her about it."

He nods. "Don't you think you should?"

Craig's right. Nikki has a say in this too.

"No matter what, I wouldn't leave you high and dry," I say. "I'd give you notice, and I'd definitely find you someone to work with."

Craig waves me off. "I'm a big boy. There're lots of guys to work with. But you asked about Vince, and I'm hearing rumors about him trying to score a new fighter. He's spreading buzz, Log. Buzz that you're out after this fight."

Once again, my feet fall to a stop along the pavement. I always knew I was replaceable, but I figured Vince would wait to replace me until I said I was done.

"You know what they say about you never having won while dating someone."

I nod.

"Vince thinks you might give it all up for her."

I say nothing. We walk back toward the house and stop to stretch. Whether I like it or not, going into the fight with Nikki on my arm could be setting me up to retire a loser. Decisions have to be made before I step into that ring.

Chapter Twenty-one

Nikki

"I didn't think I'd need my hiking boots for a date." Nor did I think I would be out of breath hiking up a trail. This is not my type of date, but I won't ruin it. Logan was so excited when he messaged from the gym earlier, telling me what to wear.

"Just a little farther and you can take them off," he says. "I do like the view though."

I look over my shoulder to see his attention on my ass. "I think it's a little early for my ass to be in your face so long."

Waking up in Logan's bed this morning felt good. Smelling him on the pillowcase, remembering his body pressed to mine. His hands exploring my body the night before. I could kick myself for not taking this step sooner.

"Hate to break it to you, but I've been staring at your ass since we met."

I wiggle my ass and he comes up behind me, pressing both hands to my ass cheeks. "If you keep doing that, we'll never make it to wherever you're leading me."

"We could make a quick pit stop," he says.

I look at the leaves and twigs. Just because I live in Alaska doesn't mean I'm at one with nature. I'm thinking Logan missed the mark on that one. Especially since it's nearing dusk, which means soon the sun will go down. I have no idea how we'll get out of here alive. But I'm trying to be optimistic and not show my crazy controlling side so early in this... whatever this is between us.

We break through the tree line and into a clearing. There's a lake surrounded by mountains, and I stare at the sky that's just starting to get the softest hues of pink and orange mixed in with the blue. It's breathtaking.

"Congratulations, you made it," Logan says and drops the bag he's carrying.

I drop the backpack he gave me and sit down, staring up. "You do know the sun is going to go down and the animals will come out?"

He opens his large backpack and pulls out a small tent. "Good thing your brother is great at directions."

"Adam?" I ask, assuming it had to be him.

He smiles and nods. "Gave me the map and told me where to go. He said we're most likely safe here."

"Most likely isn't very reassuring."

He chuckles and unfolds the tent. "Let's see if we can follow directions together." He holds up the stakes.

Yeah, this is not my forte. "I hate to break this to you after we've made it this far, but I'm guessing Adam didn't tell you I'm not really an adventurist. I don't usually partake in the outdoor adventures most Alaskans enjoy."

He laughs and hands me the tent poles. "Straighten these out. We need shelter just in case."

My gut twists at the thought of sleeping out here all by

ourselves. I mean, one bear, and we're both done. "Do you have a gun?"

He looks up at me from under his dark eyelashes and nods.

"Do you know how to use a gun?"

"No. But Adam gave me a quick lesson."

I stare blankly in disbelief. One of us will end up being shot before any bear most likely.

"I'm kidding." He takes a pole from my hand. "I know how to use one, but I am borrowing one from your brother."

"Give me more specifics. When did you use a gun last?" I hand him another pole and he slides it through the canvas slot.

"Trust me. You're safe. I'm your husband." He winks, and my stomach flips. It still feels surreal that I'll be able to sleep with this man tonight because he is indeed my husband.

"Speaking of..." I broach the subject that needs to be addressed.

"Let's wait to have that conversation until everything is set up, okay?"

I nod and we continue to put the tent up. Our first successful mission as a team. The fact it's standing is a great sign we can work together. We're losing more and more sunlight and the darker it becomes outside, the more scared I become.

Next, he digs a spot for a fire and starts one as if he's not an MMA fighter but a survivalist.

"Where did you learn all this?" I ask.

He stops teepeeing the twigs he picked up around the perimeter and looks at me. "I'm not a city boy."

"But you're not an Alaskan boy either. Didn't you say you grew up in Indiana?" I ask, bringing my legs to my chest.

"If you must know, I was a Boy Scout. Only for a short period, but—" He stops speaking.

"You're holding back on me," I say.

He shrugs. "It's embarrassing."

My stomach goes berserk with the shy smile that forms on his face over the flames. "Now you have to tell me."

He sits back on his ankles, adjusting the fire so it won't go out. "Then let's play a game. I tell you something, you tell me something."

"I don't really believe in secrets." I shrug. "So I'm game, but you're going first."

He sighs and nods. "I was in the middle of earning my forestry badge when my dad left us."

"Daddy issues too, huh?"

He shakes his head. "Not really. My mom filled in as best she could. But some of the boys started picking on me, so I quit. My mom still made me earn every badge myself, with her help. She said my dad wasn't going to ruin something I enjoyed so much, that we didn't need him anyway."

I smile, thinking of Pauline. She's such an awesome mom. I haven't seen her much since the soccer game, but she's still in town.

"I've barely been able to see her," I say.

He laughs. "She's having the time of her life in Sunrise Bay. She's never met a stranger. Anyway, that's how I know how to do this stuff. It's embarrassing."

"I think it's sweet. Why would you be embarrassed?"

He comes over and sits next to me, poking the fire with a long stick. "Because my mom forced me to earn the badges. I didn't even earn them all until I was eighteen. You can imagine how hard I hid that from any of my friends. I never would've heard the end of it."

I lay my head on his shoulder. "I think it's respectable and sexy."

He cocks an eyebrow, and I can't help the laugh that sneaks out. "Sexy?"

"Well, maybe not sexy. But I think it says a lot about you."

His lips fall to the top of my head and I close my eyes briefly at the contact. "Your turn. Tell me something embarrassing."

I rack my brain to think of something to tell him. "I don't have a lot of embarrassing stories. At least, not ones you don't already know."

His eyebrows shoot up. "Really?"

"Honest." I hold up my hand. "The only one I can really think of is that I was on this date once and during the date, we were talking about vacations and I opened my phone to show him a picture from a whale-watching tour I'd done. As I showed it to him, Molly messaged me that he'd approached her two weeks before. She screenshot a picture of him and wrote douche over the top and drew a penis coming out of his mouth."

Logan laughs. "Tell me you didn't look me up?"

I look away from the fire and shake my head. "Just the other night, but I only searched your name and the word marriage."

He runs a hand over his forehead. "Phew, thank goodness you're my first wife."

"What would I find if I did?" I hold my breath while I wait for his answer.

"You'd find out your husband lives a boring life. You'd probably see a lot of pictures of me in the ring. Some out with friends, and I'm not gonna lie, probably some women. But I'm not the lothario you think I am."

"I never outright said that."

The sun is almost down past the mountains and Logan lays out a blanket for us. "I can read between the lines when it comes to your dad. He cheated, so every man must."

I exhale loudly. "It's hard for me to trust guys in general, and with the number of temptations you must face, it's hard to conceive that you could be faithful, if I'm being honest. I've seen a lot of selfish, impulsive behavior hurt the people I care about over the years."

He turns to me, his thumb brushing along my cheek. "I always want you to be honest. It's the only way I can prove you wrong. I'm in this, Nikki, one-hundred percent."

The fire reflecting in his blue eyes draws me in. I sink farther into him, unable to deny the attraction that's been building since I woke up as his wife.

"My question is, are you one-hundred percent in this?" His voice is rough and gravelly.

"It's really hard for me. I'm still scared about getting hurt, but..." I swallow hard and take the step I need to if I ever want to move forward with my life. "I'm in this, Logan."

He smiles, and my insides warm from his happiness. "Can I ask what changed your mind last night?"

I tear my gaze away and study the fire in front of us. "Molly told me to look at our wedding pictures. And there it was... the way you were looking at me. Even though you were drunk, there was this kind and loving expression pouring out of your eyes and I finally realized I'd be an idiot to not explore this."

He captures my lips in a quick kiss. "Thank you for trusting me."

I nod, unable to speak because although I'm here to explore this, I can't help but also have my exit plan prepared.

"I have another question then," he says, and I'm scared about what he's going to ask. "Are you cool coming with me to Vegas in three weeks?"

"I thought your fight wasn't for another month?" I ask.

"I always go early for promotions and weigh-in, get my head in the game."

This is when reality will come bearing down on us. "I'll definitely be there for the fight, but I have to work. I can't go down with you right away."

He lowers me down on the blanket so he's half on top of me. "It's okay. No pressure. I just want you ringside when I win."

I wrap my arms around his neck. "Then I'll be there."

He kisses me one more time then rolls over and I'm left staring at a sky full of stars. His hand slides into mine, weaving our fingers together.

"It's beautiful," he murmurs.

"It's breathtaking," I add. "I'm not sure the last time I stargazed."

"So the hike was worth it?" He laughs and I look over at him.

"Very worth it." I squeeze his hand. "Thank you."

"Thank you, Nikki."

We're silent for a while, then he points out the Big Dipper and a few other constellations. When we're about to retire inside the tent, a shooting star falls from the sky.

"Make a wish, Nik," he says, using my shortened name and something about that feels oh so right.

I close my eyes and silently wish that this marriage works out. My eyes open to find Logan smiling at me, then he takes my head in his hand.

"Me too," he whispers and his lips land on mine.

I still worry about how I could fall for someone so fast, but I'm trying not to question logic at this point. I have to stop myself from second-guessing everything. Logan Stone isn't the man I thought he was. Not even close. He's way better.

Chapter Twenty-two

"Do your wifely duties involve pulling
splinters out of my ass?"

-Logan Stone

Logan

If someone asked me weeks ago if I thought I'd actually be successful in getting Nikki to cross that bridge with her hand in mine, I'm not sure I would've taken that bet. We still have a long way to go, but her transformation amazes me. She's taking the initiative in showing me affection now, something I wouldn't have thought possible a few weeks ago.

"You're up too early," she says, coming out of the tent and cozying up to me next to the fire.

I've never had a night like last night. Sex under the stars and a night alone in the wilderness. Add it to the list of things I never would've thought I'd do. Especially when I was growing up.

"I kind of like this outdoors thing," I say, and she laughs.

"Are you going to quit fighting and become a survivalist now?"

I wrap my arm around her shoulders, pulling her closer. "I think it might be my calling."

"Just an FYI then, I'm not an outdoorsy person."

"I figured that out last night when you wouldn't leave the tent to pee."

She giggles. "Not that I didn't fully enjoy my night last night."

I glance at her head on my shoulder. "Best night of my life."

She rolls her eyes and I put my finger under her chin to make sure she's looking into my eyes.

"Best night of my life," I repeat and place a chaste kiss on her lips.

She smiles and tips her head again to stare at the fire. "Tonight is duo night in town."

"Duo night?"

She nods. "Two businesses sort of merge together for the night and the town comes out to support them. It's just something fun."

"And you bring this up why?" I hope I know why she's bringing this up, but I don't want to assume anything.

She pushes her body into mine. "I thought we'd go together. We can out ourselves."

"Doesn't everyone already think we're out?"

She laughs. "My family knows something is up, believe me. They might act like they think we're happy, but they know this was a Vegas wedding and they know me."

I turn to face her. "You want to be an actual couple now?"

We haven't had the full conversation, and although it sounds a tad high school and juvenile, a large part of me wants to hear her say she's mine and vice versa.

"Logan, why don't you just tell me what you want?" She straddles me and puts her hands around my neck.

I look at her. "Are you really my wife?"

She holds up her left hand and wiggles her fingers. I bring it to my mouth and kiss the inside of her wrist.

"I'm going to need a verbal affirmation."

"Yes, I'm your wife," she says before kissing me. "Although I will admit this seems weird that we went from strangers to married and dating, but we're married."

"It is unusual, but it feels right, don't you think?"

She laughs. "Never in a million years did I think I'd find an MMA fighter who believes in signs and fate and marry him the night I met him."

She presses her body to mine and my hands fall to her ass, grinding my hard length along her core. She starts grinding of her own accord and my lips seek out her neck. It's hard to imagine ever getting enough of her.

Abruptly, she slides back on my legs and looks around for a second. Adam told me that we probably needed to get out of here by early morning because hikers will start showing up. It's still pretty early, so I have time to take her right here.

She slides off my legs and drops to her knees in front of the fire, her eyes never leaving me. "Someone is wishing me good morning." Her hands go to the sides of my shorts and I rise up from the log to help her take them off.

"He was feeling pretty neglected." I run my hand through her hair. The fact her messy ponytail has more hair out than in and she feels comfortable like this in my presence makes me happy. This is something I've wanted in a relationship for so long. Authenticity.

She runs her palms up my thighs and grabs my length with one hand. "Let me make it up to him."

Her small hand grips my dick, and she pumps it a few times, up and down, twirling around the top.

"Fuck, that feels good." My head rolls back between my

shoulder blades for a moment before the urge to see her taking me in her mouth is more important.

She leans forward, her tongue parting her lips, and I watch with fascination as she moves closer to my dick. At first, she licks up the length of me, her mouth surrounding the tip, then she's swallowing me down her throat.

"Fucking hell, you're good at that."

She glances up at me through her thick eyelashes and smiles, swirling her tongue along the tip again before she eases me down her throat, sucking and pumping.

My hands have nowhere to go, so they fist in her hair. My hips rock, loving how deep she's taking me. She knows way too much about how to get me off and I'm riding on the edge, not wanting this feeling to go away. Not so soon. But her free hand cradles my balls, and I can't for the life of me hold out any longer.

"I'm coming," I say, my fingers clenching in her blonde strands. She stays in place and I take that as a sign that she'll be swallowing, which makes any small amount of willpower I had left crash land.

"And here we have this gorgeous clearing where we'll stop for a snack," a woman's voice says.

Nikki lifts her head and my cum sprays her in the eye. She rears back and I rock forward, my ass sliding along the wood log.

We both look left to see a group of girls and their leader dressed in green, but the smell of hair burning takes my attention back to Nikki. Smoke's coming from behind her head. I tackle her to the ground, and she smacks me on the back.

"The girls. Logan, get off of me!" she yells.

"Your hair is on fire," I mumble.

"Miss Hartford, what are those two doing?"

The woman screeches at my naked ass up in the air.

"My hair!" Nikki turns her head and comes away with singed strands.

Fuck, how did our amazing night turn so disastrous?

"Excuse me, you two, I have impressionable girls here." The leader stomps over to us.

I get off Nikki, quick to grab my pants and hide behind the tent until I'm fully covered, but the pain in my ass is killing me. Nikki quickly uses her shirt to wipe her face.

"I'm so sorry," Nikki says. "My husband and I were just waking up."

I come from around the tent and put my arm around Nikki, looking at the back of her head. She's not going to be happy. A few inches of hair will have to be cut off.

"I see that. You know camping is prohibited here, don't you?" She digs into her backpack and pulls out a cell phone.

Shit. Adam told me that, but said we'd be fine if we were out early this morning. I didn't think he meant the ass crack of dawn though.

I do not need this being reported anywhere. Not when Nikki and I are finally getting somewhere. If she sees the media storm that can come from being with someone like me, she's sure to leave me.

"Ma'am, this was an honest mistake. I tried to do something romantic for my wife." I approach her, leaving Nikki near the tent.

"What you two were doing was *not* romantic," the woman says, glaring at me.

The girls all giggle behind her, one saying what she saw and the others chiming in.

"I understand what you must be thinking, but please, what can we do to make this right? I can buy your entire collection of cookies."

Nikki comes over. "They aren't Girl Scouts, Logan. They're in survivalist training."

Could have fooled me. "Oh, sorry."

"Yes, we build fires and hunt and fish. Speaking of, did you know that fire you started is against code for this area?" One of the girls comes up with an open book. "We should call the park ranger and get them fined."

Miss Hartford poises her phone in front of her, staring at me.

I hold up my hands. "Okay, okay. We made a few mistakes."

"Go ahead and call, my brother's a ranger," Nikki says.

I look over my shoulder and see her standing there with her arms crossed and hip cocked.

"No!" I hold up my hand. "Listen, you look like tough girls, but how about you come down to Pump It Up one day and I can show you a few moves to defend yourselves?"

The girl who probably knows the book she's reading by heart looks at her leader. "It would be good for us to learn some self-defense."

The woman looks at me. "How do I know you're qualified?"

"Qualified? He's Logan Stone," Nikki chimes in again.

I wince. I was gonna try to keep that under wraps until they agreed.

"Logan Stone?" the girl asks and looks behind her, where the other three girls have pulled out their phones.

Once they've obviously got an image of me on their phones, they all giggle and show one another. The one with blonde braids brings her phone up to the girl with the leader.

She reads it then looks at me, and I feel as though I'm about to be interrogated by the world's youngest federal agent. "He is, Miss Hartford. He's at the end of his career, but he's telling the truth."

"End of his career?" Nikki comes up to me and swings her arm through mine. "He holds the title, and he fights again soon where he'll keep the title. End of his career?" she scoffs. "Check your facts."

"It says he's thirty-four." The girl looks at Nikki like *duh*.

I pat Nikki's hand. I appreciate her sticking up for me, but the girl is right. I'm nearing the end of my career if I want to go out on top.

"Well, it only means I'm more knowledgeable, doesn't it?" I say.

The whole group looks me over.

I'm starting to feel a little insecure until Miss Hartford sighs and nods. "Okay. But you two need to pack up your stuff and leave. Make sure you put out that fire."

"Do you own this piece of land?" Nikki asks.

I laugh and put my body in front of hers, leading her back to our tent. "Thank you. I'm at Pump It Up every day from one to three, so just stop by and let me know when you want to plan some time with the girls."

"Logan, we don't have to leave. Adam will come and tell them."

I shake my head. "Let's just pack up and get home. Plus, you need to see someone about your hair."

She touches the back. "How am I going to explain this? I can't very well tell people that I burned off my hair giving you a blow job."

"We also have another problem," I tell her.

"What?"

"Do your wifely duties involve pulling splinters out of my ass?"

Her eyes widen. "Seriously?"

I nod and her head falls back in laughter. I could watch her laugh all day, but I shake my head and get started folding the tent up.

After we have everything packed, we head back to my truck.

"Hey," I say to her once we're secure in the cab.

"Yeah?"

"Thanks for sticking up for me back there."

She might not know how much that means to me, but it does. Rarely in my life has anyone gone to bat for me, and it only proves my gut was right to follow her up here.

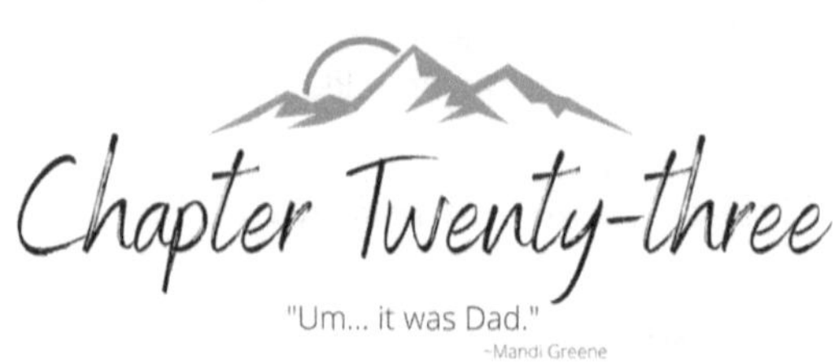

Chapter Twenty-three

Nikki

"This isn't something I thought my wife would be doing until at least ten years into the marriage," Logan says, lying on his stomach on the bed.

"Just hold still." I pluck another splinter out of his ass. "I'd rather do it now when your ass looks like this than when it's all saggy."

"Are you suggesting my ass is gonna be saggy in ten years?"

"Well, you are at the end of your career," I joke, laughing so he knows I'm only kidding. The way his eyes were so grateful and caring when he thanked me for sticking up for him... I've never felt so appreciated for doing such a small thing.

"Funny. Let's remember the vows, for better or worse."

I pluck out another one.

"Ouch!"

"Sorry." I cringe. "Isn't that the problem though? I don't remember the vows."

"Just another reason for us to repeat them."

I freeze with the tweezers over another splinter. "What?"

He tries to glance over his shoulder but can't. "I want us to renew our vows at some point."

I grab another splinter. "Like when?"

"Relax. Not until my fight is over and we've dated for a little bit."

I laugh because surely that sentence has never been said before. "Let's get all these splinters out and then my hair cut. One problem at a time."

I hear the downstairs door open and then, "Logan!" I tense for a moment.

"Busy, Mom, come back later," he yells back, and the tension leaves my muscles.

Of course it's Pauline. I need to stop thinking some woman is going to come in and throw a landmine into our situation.

"You're never busy for me, unless Nikki's with you." I hear her footsteps on the stairs.

"She is with me."

"Hi, Pauline," I say with the hope it will keep her out of here. Not that it's my ass on display.

"Oh, sweetie, you're who I wanted to see. There's all this talk about this duo night." She walks into the room and rears back in horror. "You don't have hemorrhoids again, do you?"

"I'm tapping out," I say.

"Jesus, Mom, I've never had hemorrhoids. And please leave." He throws his head into the pillow and screams. "I swear, Nikki, I've never had hemorrhoids."

Pauline strolls into the room and looks over my shoulder. "Really? I swear it was you. Maybe that was Bert. He was an old boyfriend." She touches my arm. "Always had one health problem or another."

"He did have two heart attacks," Logan says.

"And I nursed him back to health after each one," Pauline says and rolls her eyes.

Their banter as son and mom is cute.

"What happened here?" She points at Logan's ass.

"He has splinters," I say, placing the blanket over his bare ass.

"Don't hide him on my account. I wiped that butt once upon a time." Pauline sits in the chair in the corner.

Logan looks at her. "Can you please leave? This is a husband-and-wife moment."

Pauline's face lights up. "Oh, so you're husband and wife. I mean, I took it as a good sign that she'd hover over your butt."

My face slowly heats.

"I finally wore her down." Logan tries again to look at me, but he can't until I finish with this.

"I knew he would. He's a charmer." Pauline beams. "In a good way, Nikki. I'd never steer you wrong."

"Well, thank you. It's a little surreal and weird, but we're going with it."

"Obviously. You should've had Craig take the splinters out. You're ruining all the sexuality with marriage."

I shake my head. "It's okay. I don't mind."

"Want to tell me how it happened?" She props one foot up on the edge of the chair.

Logan groans. "Please leave, Mom."

"After you tell me how it happened."

I pinch Logan to say I'll be mad if he tells her, and he sighs into the pillow.

"She won't stop until we tell her," he mumbles.

"I have a feeling this is a good story," she says, rubbing her hands together.

I smile at her. "Logan took me camping. In the middle of the night, he had to go to the bathroom, fell on a log, and voila—splinters."

She points at me and laughs, standing from her chair. "Oh, you're a tricky one. I don't believe you for a second. There's an interesting story behind this one, I know it." She pats me on the shoulder. "I'll be downstairs talking to Iris about herbs that will help with inflammation from training."

After Pauline leaves, Logan says, "She's gonna figure out what really happened."

I remove the blanket and take out the final two splinters. "I need to get some cream."

I head into the master bath with the hopes of finding some ointment. Lucky me, whoever manages the Linville house has a first aid kit stocked in the bathroom. When I return, Logan's on his back.

"Roll over, hubby, I've got something that's going to soothe that ass of yours."

He smiles at me. "That sounds dangerous."

"Don't worry, no hemorrhoid cream." I circle my finger for him to roll over.

"I'm serious, I've never had hemorrhoids," he says, his face red as he rolls over.

"Don't worry, that's where I draw the line. I'm not sticking any cream in places I have to spread your ass cheeks to get to."

"Nor would I ever ask you to."

I put the ointment on my hands and rub it over his butt cheeks, which I have to say are pure muscle. "You might be a bit sore."

He rolls over and pulls up his pants, signaling for me to climb on top of him.

"That's what got us in trouble in the first place," I say before kissing his lips.

He wraps his hand around the back of my neck and keeps me pressed to his lips, sliding his tongue into my mouth. We kiss as though Pauline isn't waiting on us downstairs, and the tingling between my legs commences as it always does now when he's near. Then the smell of burned hair wafts to my nostrils and I remember I need to get to Posey's to get this fixed.

I draw back. "I have to go get my hair done. I'm crossing my fingers no one is there when I arrive."

He kisses me one last time. "So duo night tonight... what time do we leave?"

I love that he remembers and seems to be looking forward to it. "Sixish. You can invite your mom if you'd like."

"No way, it's our coming out." A mischievous smile crosses his lips, and my stomach reacts as always.

Damn, now I've gone and done it. I've really fallen for this guy.

I ENTER FRINGE, my sister Posey's, hair salon, surprised to see every other Greene female in attendance. All of them are in the waiting area, pretending to read magazines.

"Cute, guys." I roll my eyes.

Mandi tips down the corner of her magazine. "Emergency haircut?"

I say nothing and walk to the back where Posey's coming out from the back room.

"Hey, Nik, have a seat." She points at a shampoo station. "So, what's the emergency?"

I glance at my family at the front and back at her, then I take off the hat I've shoved all my hair into and turn around to show her.

She gasps. "What the hell happened?"

"Lower your voice," I whisper. "I just want a change," I say loud enough for my sisters and Chevelle to hear.

"Change, my ass." Chevelle has no qualms and comes to the back. "We already heard. Miss Hartford was my survivalist leader." I stare blankly at her, so she continues. "She called me this morning to ask if Logan is really an MMA fighter and if my sister Nikki is married to him."

I groan. Seriously, I hate how small this town is sometimes. Before I moved here at fourteen, I had no idea there was such a thing as a survivalist.

"I love Miss Hartford. Though it's a little scary that she's still doing it, no?" Posey asks, getting the sink ready. "She had us watching what she thought was a deer and it was a moose. She kept blowing a duck call and the thing almost stampeded us." Posey shakes her head as though the memory is vivid.

"Yeah, I thought she'd have packed it in by now, but I have a feeling there's no one to take it over," Chevelle says. "So you burned your hair from having sex too close to the fire." She shrugs. "What's the big deal? You're not the first."

Warm water coasts over my head and I close my eyes from the sensation. "Well, I don't much care for being caught. Those girls are young and impressionable."

Chevelle scoffs. "Please, the leader of them, Darcie, is Fran's granddaughter. Once she's old enough, she'll probably take over the group."

"She's a know-it-all just like Fran," I say.

Fran and her walking gang have eyes everywhere and they like to put their nose in other people's business, but I've never had a problem with them. She and Chevelle once had it out over a water excursion she was setting up for tourists though. Fran said there were too many kayaks and someone was going to be killed by a fishing boat. Chevelle's never forgiven her.

"All I have to say is your mother-in-law is awesome. She's been helping me in the restaurant in the mornings," Mandi says. "Everyone loves her. She's started reading tarot cards there before dinner."

I look at Posey and she nods and says, "Did mine last night. Says my Prince Charming will come to town like a thunderstorm so strong it'll make quakes."

I nod. Are my sisters really believing all this?

"She told me that mine's from Sunrise Bay. How boring is that?" Chevelle leans back in the other shampoo chair. "All the guys in this town suck."

"Cam," Posey says with a fake cough. "Wouldn't that be hilarious?"

We all laugh because those two fight like siblings. Maybe because Cam practically grew up in the Greene house. Every time he and Chevelle are together, they find something to argue about.

"Bite your tongue. Never!"

We all laugh again.

"What about you, Mandi?" I ask.

She shakes her head. "Nah, I haven't had her do mine yet."

Posey finishes shampooing me, and we go over to her chair. "Enough about that, tell us about Logan. If the rumors are true, you two are getting it on in the woods."

"We're married. Married people have sex." I shrug it off as though it's nothing.

"We're not stupid, Nik. You came back here without him after you were first married." Mandi sits in the chair next to mine while Chevelle sits in the other one.

"Come on, just be honest. Marla's not here." Chevelle twirls in her chair. Sometimes I wonder if she'll ever completely grow up.

I sigh. "We're giving it a go. I mean, we're dating."

Posey looks at me through the mirror. "That's great! I'm so happy for you. He seems like a great guy."

My phone rings in my purse and I'm sure it must be my mom asking for details too. "Can you grab it, Mandi? If it's Mom, tell her I'll call her back."

Posey cuts my hair as Mandi digs in my purse but can't find my phone. The ringing stops and we all wait because usually she'll try one of my sisters if the one she wants doesn't answer. We all stare at one another when no one else's phone rings.

"Must not have been Mom. See who it was?" I say.

Mandi finally finds my phone and stares at the screen, her smile dimming. "Um... it was Dad."

Posey glances at me in the mirror, then dips her head down to concentrate on cutting my hair. My stomach sours immediately.

What the hell does my dad want? Usually I only hear from him on holidays and my birthday.

I shake my head. Of course, he probably wants to meet his new son-in-law, the professional MMA fighter, so he can brag to all his friends.

I haven't really given any thought to what my dad might think of my marriage. Besides the trust issues I carry around, he doesn't really factor into my daily life. But I've got something that's worth something to him now. Of course he's calling. How did I just realize this now?

180

Chapter Twenty-four

"Jed, go inside."
~Hank Greene

Logan

"My ass is going to need some lovin' tonight," I say to Nikki on our way into town for this duo night she's so excited about.

Craig snickers and Nikki quirks an eyebrow. "I take it Craig knows what happened?"

"My training suffered a little bit today."

"A little?" Craig shakes his head. "I kicked his legs out from under him and you'd think he broke his tailbone."

They both laugh at my expense.

"It was a lot of splinters," Nikki says.

"The whole reason for needing some lovin'." I take Nikki's hand as we approach the square, and much to my satisfaction, she doesn't pull away.

"Not sure what you want me to do," she says.

"I don't wanna hear what he wants you to do." With a laugh, Craig walks ahead as if he's not with us, then he holds up and joins us again.

We enter the square, and there are more people than usual here. From what Nikki says, Handyman Haven and The Grind are working together tonight, so they've put on an exhibit outside in the square where George, the owner of Handyman Haven, will show people how to do some rehab project while Zoe from The Grind serves coffee and hot chocolate.

Immediately, we run into Nikki's mom and Hank.

"Hey, you two." Marla gives us each a kiss on the cheek and a hug.

"Marla, this is my trainer, Craig. Craig, this is Nikki's mom, Marla," I introduce them. "And her stepdad, Hank."

"You up for watching the rehab project?" Craig asks Hank.

"Nah, I could do that with my eyes closed."

Marla puts her arm around her husband's waist and pats his stomach. "Hank is the town fix-it man."

Her words get my mind swirling about an idea I had for Nikki. Although she and I haven't talked at all about where we'll live after this fight, I sense the majority of our time will be spent up here, which is fine with me. I'm starting to like this small town. But Nikki needs a place to record her podcasts, and since I have no idea where we'll live after tourist season, I need to set something up for her soon.

"Hank, can I talk to you for a minute?" I ask.

"Sure, you can," Marla answers for Hank.

Hank laughs at his wife. "Of course."

"We'll be watching the redo. I see George brought up guests to make it more entertaining." Marla points in the direction of the crowd.

"I'll meet you over there." I kiss Nikki on the cheek and step away with Hank.

He and I weave out of the crowd and end up outside

Truth or Dare Brewery. It's filled with wall-to-wall people too.

"You enjoying your first duo night?" Hank asks. "It's more about getting the people out to socialize and spotlighting some businesses to help with exposure."

"I think it's a great idea, and yeah, so far I'm enjoying my time in Sunrise Bay."

Hank nods and waves to a few people who pass by and call to him by name. What must it be like to know everyone in town? "That's good. Sometimes people get overwhelmed in a town like this where everyone knows everything. Like the unfortunate incident with you and Nikki this morning."

My eyes bulge out of my head. "So people heard about that?"

He shrugs and nods.

"How's your ass, Stone?" Jed, Nikki's brother, comes out of Truth or Dare Brewery.

"Lower your voice, Jed," Hank says.

"Why? Everyone knows already. Miss Hartford has the biggest mouth. You'd have been better off with the Gossip Brigade finding you two. They might've had sympathy for you, being men and all." Jed laughs.

Hank gives Jed a look, but it doesn't stop him. I assume not much does.

"Anyway, I called you over here to ask a question," I say to Hank.

"He's the stepdad, but our dad is a cocksucker, so you can ask me for Nikki's hand." Jed comes to stand with us.

That wasn't what I was going to ask Hank. "Um..."

"Jed, go inside," Hank says.

"Sure, one thing though. I hate hearing rumors about my sister being naked in the woods. If you two could keep it behind closed doors, it'd be much appreciated." Jed dramatically shakes his entire body as though it skeeves him out to know his sister has sex.

The sound of someone banging on the window pulls our attention to the brewery. Molly's standing there with her hands on her hips.

"Jed! I am not working this place alone. Get in here." She says it so loudly, we have no problem hearing her through the glass.

Jed walks backward. "Whatever happened to respecting your boss, am I right?" He disappears back inside.

"You have to excuse Jed—"

"It's fine. I should probably ask for Nikki's hand, but I haven't had any contact with her father. From the sounds of it, she doesn't much either."

Hank's lips purse and he shakes his head. "The kids were old enough to know what happened between him and their mom, and they still harbor ill feelings toward Jeff. But I can get you in contact with him if you'd like."

"Yeah, maybe, but that's not the reason I wanted to talk to you."

He waves to a few more people and some of them say hello to me too. Hank smiles at me. "Becoming a regular, huh?" He laughs at what I imagine is my surprised look. "What do you need?"

"Nikki's talked about wanting to do a podcast. Since we don't own the Linville house and I have no idea where we might move, I'm thinking about building a small studio for her in an office somewhere."

Hank's smile grows wider, and he pats me on the back. "I have just the spot. I heard the small shop next to Pump It Up will be coming up for purchase in a week or so. It's been vacant for years. Was once our small newspaper office, but they can't afford the rent, so they're working out of their houses now. You might be interested in that."

"And as far as getting it soundproofed and stuff?"

"Are you asking me to do it?" Hank asks.

"Yeah. Or if you know a guy."

He's quiet for a moment, and I wonder if I messed up somehow. I just want to show Nikki how much I want her to succeed.

"Can I offer you some advice?" Hank asks.

I nod.

"Come, let's walk."

I walk in stride with Hank, and he leads us away from the town square, taking us toward the bay.

"I've done my research on you, Logan." He glances at me and shrugs. "I had to be sure I was protecting Nikki. And I know you don't have a father, so you can take my fatherly advice however you want."

My stomach squirms. I respect Hank, but I never needed a father growing up and I sure don't need one now.

"Nikki's dad, Jeff, is pretty rich. He doesn't lack for much. And when the whole thing went down between him and Marla, he thought he could buy his kids' love. They each got a brand-new car at sixteen. They were given credit cards to use how they wanted. It's how he shows his love and it's part of the reason things didn't work out."

I nod. "I understand completely. I don't wanna buy Nikki's love. I want to earn it. Plus, I don't want her to be with me just for my money."

He pats my shoulder. "That's why I'm going to give you this advice. I'll chip in and help with the studio podcast, especially since you're not knowledgeable about building, but if you put in the blood, sweat, and tears yourself, I suspect it will mean much more to her. Thinking of her is one thing. Acting and executing it yourself is another in a woman's eyes."

I stop for a moment and think about what he's saying. He's right. Paying someone to do things for her isn't the same as me doing it for her. I'm going to have to roll up my sleeves and put in some sweat equity.

"It's just my opinion and I could be off base. Maybe I'm just old now and women don't care, but Marla always makes sure to thank me when it's me who hangs the picture for her instead of someone from my crew, if you know what I mean?" He winks.

I force a smile because I'm not cool envisioning them in bed. "Thanks, Hank. It means a lot that you took the time to talk to me."

"You're my son-in-law now. Our door is open anytime."

We walk back toward the crowd again and find Nikki with Marla and my mom. The two older women are carrying on, laughing and talking over one another.

"What did I miss?" I whisper to Nikki, who looks relieved to see me.

A tight smile lands on her lips. "They're just laughing at our mishap, then they started sharing stories of their own mishaps."

Glad I missed that conversation.

"Want a coffee?" I ask.

"Love one," she says, taking my hand and pulling me away. "Pauline, Mom, we'll see you later."

She drags me over to the table that sells the coffee, and I spot Craig talking with the owner of The Grind. At least he's not bored.

"Let's go for a walk," Nikki says.

"You don't want to see the home improvement show?"

She laughs. "You should probably know, I broke Jed's

thumb with a hammer once while he was holding the nail. They've banned me from tools ever since."

"I'll have to do all the home improvement projects, is that what you're telling me?"

"I don't see you as the handy type either. I think we'll need contractors on call."

Wait until I prove her wrong.

"I wanted to talk to you about something," she says after a beat of silence. Her humorous tone has shifted to a more serious one and alarms flash in my head.

"What's up?"

"My dad called me today," she says.

I release the breath. "Is he mad? I should probably ask him for your hand."

She stops short and places her hand on my arm. "No. You don't have to ask him for anything. He lost that right a long time ago. But I have to call him back. And I have a funny suspicion he's reaching out for something to do with you."

"Me?"

She takes a sip of her coffee. "You're a celebrity. My dad travels to Vegas all the time. I'm thinking he probably wants tickets to your fight."

I shrug. "No problem. I'd love to meet your dad anyway. I'll talk to Vince."

She doesn't say anything for a moment. "I guess he should meet you at some point. Just do me one favor?"

"Say the word." I stop and turn her to face me, bringing my hands behind her back.

"Don't let him talk you into anything."

My forehead wrinkles. "Like what?"

"Just promise me, you get him the tickets and that's it."

I kiss her forehead. "Promise. But he is your dad."

She shakes her head and pulls away. "He's my biological dad. That's all. He's never had my interests at heart. Ever."

I take our coffees and throw them in the nearby garbage container. Then I pull her to me, hoping to shelter her from some of the pain that's still being rained down on her from her dad.

Chapter Twenty-five

Nikki

Talking to Logan about my dad was embarrassing but a necessity. After I finish the morning show, all I can think about is what my dad will ask me when I call him back this afternoon. I'm purposely waiting, hoping I'll get to leave a voice message because he's in a meeting or something.

Leaving the station, I stop at The Grind for a coffee and sit down at a table for two. Logan's training today, so I might as well just get this conversation over with. I pick up the phone and press my dad's name, sipping my coffee.

"Nik!" he answers as though we're best friends. "I was just about to call you back."

"Sorry, I've been busy."

"I know. I heard the news. How could you not invite your old man to your wedding?" He laughs. "Kidding, I know it was an impromptu occasion."

"Yeah," I say.

"Logan Stone... so does that mean you're now Nikki Stone?"

His questions bring up something I haven't thought of until now. I've never considered changing my name. Maybe because we're dating while married.

"I'm still Nikki Greene."

"That's my independent girl." He acts as though he's proud of me for not taking the name, but he would've thrown a fit if my mom or his other two wives didn't take on Greene. Plus, he's a chauvinist who believes he makes the money and his wife should stay at home.

"What did you need?" I ask to get this conversation going.

"I'm going to be in Vegas around the time of Logan's fighting Rinaldo. I thought maybe the three of us could go to dinner? My treat, of course."

"Dinner?" That isn't what I expected. I thought for sure he'd want to take his friends to the fight. Show off his clout with ringside seats because his daughter's married to the fighter.

Now that I care more for Logan, the thought of sitting there and watching him bleed in the ring makes me nauseated.

"Yeah. Celebrate, since I know he'll win," he says.

"So you don't want to go to the fight?"

He's quiet for a moment and I'm surprised, because usually he has the lines ready to go. "Well, I thought I'd sit next to you, since from the look of the pictures I saw online, you don't like fighting."

"So just you then?" I turn the coffee cup in a circle on the table.

"Your uncles are dying to go too."

"Uncles?" My dad's an only child, but I know who he's talking about. I just want to make him say it.

"Todd and Eddie. They're the ones who told me about the news—and I had to act like I knew, of course. I know things are strained between us, Nik, but I'm your father. I deserved to know you got married."

I sip my coffee. "It's been a whirlwind. You want three tickets then?"

"Yeah, but I told Todd and Eddie I'm taking you two to dinner afterward and they'll have to entertain themselves."

"I'll talk to Logan. I'm not sure about dinner. We'll have to see after the fight is over. Logan might not want to go out."

"Totally understandable."

He'd probably prefer it if Logan doesn't want to.

"I just want to meet the man who stole my daughter's heart." He laughs. "I gotta admit, I never thought I'd see the day."

"Well, I never thought I'd see the day you got married for the third time, but there you are with Jeanie. She won't be coming up to Vegas with you, will she?"

I know the answer is no. He'll leave the wife at home and come up with his buddies.

He used to tell me that I needed to hold my tongue and I should respect him. He's at least stopped pretending we'll ever have a normal relationship.

"The twins have school, and she hates to leave them."

"I'll talk to Logan and get back to you." I'd like to end this conversation now before he further ruins my day.

"Sounds great. Love you, Nik," he says.

"Bye, Dad."

I hang up and stare out the window of The Grind, watching tourists move about the town. The families hold my attention longer than normal, and I consider what my future looks like with Logan. We've never discussed kids or my name changing or where we'll live once he's done with this fight. There's so much that needs to be settled between us.

As though Logan can hear when I'm thinking of him, he and Craig stroll into The Grind, both sweaty messes with gym bags slung over their shoulders. I'll admit, it's kind of awesome to have a husband who stays so in shape. Logan spots me and leaves Craig with Zoe at the register.

"Hey," he says, sitting down and sliding his chair close to me. He leans in for a kiss, but I push his head back, leaving me with a handful of sweat.

I run it down a napkin and he laughs. "What are you doing here?"

He picks up my coffee and sips it, cringing at the sugar.

I steal it back. "Then get your own."

He laughs. "My manager called and said he's coming into town."

"Vince?" I clarify.

He nods.

"Why?" My first impression of Vince wasn't a great one. Logan has a lot of faith in him, but I don't know. I don't get the feeling that Vince has Logan's best interests in mind.

"Because he wants to check up on me. I'm his paycheck."

I frown because I don't like that and it's exactly what I'm talking about, but I don't feel it's my place to tell Logan I think his manager is using him. God knows Vince has been with Logan longer than I have.

As if he can hear my thoughts though, Logan says, "It's just business. People use people." He shrugs as though it is what it is and nothing's going to change.

"Speaking of people using people, I called my dad back."

His eyes widen. "And?"

"He wants three tickets to the fight and says he wants to take us out to dinner afterward."

He cringes. "That's nice and I'll get him tickets next to you, but I'm not sure about dinner. Depends how things go and how I feel afterward."

I smile, thinking about being alone in his suite again now that we're an actual couple. "That's pretty much what I told him."

He leans in. "Kiss me."

He's less sweaty now and I'm a sucker for those eyes, so I pucker my lips. He doesn't wait a second before his lips are on mine and his tongue is in my mouth.

Someone clears their throat and I pull away.

"You two have an entire house, and you pick a coffee shop to make out in?" Craig sits down with a muffin and a coffee.

Logan stares at the muffin. "You're going to eat that in front of me?"

Craig pushes it my way. "Zoe made me take it. Here you go, Nikki. Neither of us can eat it." Craig sips his coffee.

"Do you have to make weight too?" I ask, and he looks over at Logan.

"It's moral support," Craig says.

I'm just about to take a bite of the muffin when I look at Logan. "Should I be eating differently in front of you? I'm sorry."

Logan shakes his head. "No, I like to watch you enjoy things."

"Ew... get a room." Craig tips the chair back, leaving two legs on the floor. "Question, Nikki, is Zoe single?"

I smile because Craig is cute and, although older than Logan, younger than Zoe. "She is, and she's amazing."

"Thanks." He stands and goes back over to see Zoe at the

counter. Since it's midmorning, the place isn't packed, so he leans over the counter and I see that Zoe can't stop smiling.

Love it.

I'm interrupted from watching them when the door opens, and Vince stands there with his arms open wide. "I'm here to bring you home."

The word home coming out of Vince scares me when I think of all those unanswered questions that came to mind only a short time ago. Where is Logan's home now?

That nauseous feeling in my stomach that was just beginning to go away after speaking with my dad stirs back to life. I place my hand on Logan's thigh and he covers my hand with his as though we're a united front.

"Hey, Vince," Logan says.

Vince stops at Craig and pats him on the back, pretending he's going to hit him. I'm fairly sure Craig could get Vince in a chokehold in three seconds flat if he wanted to, but Craig is a good enough sport to play along. Then Vince tells Zoe what to get him and, without paying, struts over to us. The guy looks as if he just came out of the late eighties but forgot his Members Only jacket in his T-bird.

"The newlyweds!" Vince comes over to me, leaning down to kiss me on the cheek.

Remind me to wash that cheek when I get home.

He does some kind of man-hug thing with Logan before he sits in Craig's spot. "So how is married life treating you guys?" Vince props one foot up on his other knee, leaning back as though he owns the place.

Logan glances at me, smiling wide, then back at Vince. "Great."

"You've managed to stay out of the press, I see."

"No one followed us up here. They must not know where to find us," I say.

Vince rolls his eyes. "They know where you are. I just think a lot of people aren't willing to come up here."

Logan squeezes my hand. I'm starting to really dislike Vince.

I collect my things. "I should probably get going."

"That's for the best, because I have to talk to Logan about a few things." Vince's foot drops on the floor and he leans forward.

"I'm going to walk her out." Logan stands and takes my hand.

"Didn't mean to make you run off, Nik," Vince says.

The fact he used my nickname grates on my last nerve.

"I have plenty of things to do. Have a great flight back." I have no idea when he's leaving, but I'm hoping it's tonight.

"Oh, I'm staying until Logan goes back to Vegas. We have to go over some of the promotional things. You know, so he can keep his career thriving."

I feel like according to Vince, we're on opposing sides when it comes to Logan.

"Let's just go." Logan's hand on the small of my back urges me out of the coffee shop.

Once we're outside and the sun beams down on us, I sigh.

Logan places his finger under my chin and brings my face up to look at him. "Don't give him a second thought. All he cares about is the money from the fight."

I nod, lips pressed together tightly.

"I'm going to talk to him about the way he's talking to you. It's unacceptable, but I figured you didn't want to be there when I did."

He's right. Not that I'm shy about confrontation, but Vince makes me feel like an unwanted distraction. Maybe to him, I am, but not to Logan.

"Can we talk tonight?" I ask. Everything in me is telling me to run before things fall apart, but this man is my husband, and I made a commitment to treat him as such. Which means communicating with him when I feel uneasy about what's to come.

Logan tilts his head.

"Nothing big. Just you go back to Vegas soon and I want to see where we stand, get prepared for any changes."

He places a light kiss to my lips. "You got it."

"Thanks."

"You don't have to thank me, Nikki, I'm your husband."

I sigh at his declaration. He really does take this seriously. "See you tonight."

"See you." He kisses me one more time.

I turn away, walking back toward the house. I wish I could get rid of this feeling in my gut that the happiness between us is about to be tested. As much as Logan has reassured me, I can't shake it. Maybe there is something to listening to your gut like Logan says.

Chapter Twenty-six

Logan

walk back into The Grind, ready to give Vince a piece of my mind, but he's on the phone, laughing with someone. When I sit down, Craig glances over and hurries to tell Zoe bye so he can join us. He can always tell when something's wrong with me. Which happens with Vince a lot, at least these days.

Politely waiting for Vince to get off the phone, I wait until our eyes meet. He must see something in my face, because he sits up straighter and his laugh dies before he tells the person on the line that he has to call them back.

"Sorry, I got word about Dale Campbell looking for a manager," Vince says.

I lean back in my chair. "So the rumor is true? You're looking to take on someone else?" He opens his mouth, but before he can answer, I put up my hand. "First, let's discuss the way you talk to my wife."

"Wife?" He points at me then looks at Craig with an

expression of 'listen to this guy.' "A little quick to be her protector."

"Vince." Craig shakes his head, but that won't shut Vince up.

"She is my wife. We're together." I whisper so no one overhears us.

"Together? Of course you are. You came here on your fucking white horse and bought her a bunch of shit. We've been over this, Log, she's using you."

I inhale a deep breath and stand. "If you want to continue talking about this, we're doing it somewhere else."

I burst through the doors of The Grind, Vince and Craig right behind me. I don't stop until I'm at the storefront I bought to reno for Nikki's podcast. I've been working as much as I can on it without Nikki's knowledge, and Craig has been helping me during our breaks. I took to heart what Hank said, and after he showed me a few things, I got started.

The three of us walk inside, and I tell the crew I hired to do the soundproofing—since I want it done right—to take a break. They leave, staring at all of us. They can probably tell that none of us are happy right now.

After they leave, I turn the lock on the door. "Vince, you've been my manager a long fucking time and I'd hate for our relationship to go south because you're acting like a jealous girlfriend."

He holds his hands in the air. "What's this place?" he asks as if he didn't hear me and looks around.

"It's none of your business," I say, then I get mad at myself because the hell with what he thinks. "Actually, this is a studio for Nikki to do her podcast."

"You have to be shittin' me. You bought her a place to do a podcast and you're what, redoing it for her? A bit much, isn't it?" He walks around as if he's foreman of a construction crew.

"I want my wife to have the best. Nothing wrong with that." I shrug.

He purses his lips. "What does this mean? Is this your home now? Alaska? Really, Log?"

I've yet to broach the subject with Nikki for fear she'll push me away or I'll say something that scares her. Things are good between us right now, and in reality, this studio will be hers whether our marriage survives or not. But I hope that I'm next door, training at the gym, while she's recording her podcast and we meet back at our shared house for an afternoon quickie. Hell, I'll take her in the back room here happily.

"I don't know yet. I have to talk to Nikki still."

"You're throwing your entire career away for a piece of ass?"

Craig puts his hand on Vince's chest, but I'm already there, pushing Vince to the wall. "She's not a piece of ass. She's my wife."

Vince puts his hands in the air. "Jesus, Log, I didn't mean to disrespect her. I'm just taken by surprise. I leave you here for a bit and now you're so..."

I release him. "I'm a husband, and I will not tolerate anyone speaking about my wife like that."

He nods a few times. "Okay. Okay. I'm sorry."

"Better." I nod.

"The place is nice." He forces a smile as he looks around.

"Yeah, I've done a lot of the work myself."

"I had no idea you were handy." He jabs me with his fist in the upper arm.

I knew he'd change his attitude once he saw how serious I am about Nikki. Vince has always seen my girlfriends as a problem. That somehow they change me and not for the better. But he hasn't been here to see me with Nikki, so maybe I should cut him a bit of slack.

I sit down in one of the chairs and nod toward the other two. "Then let's sit and actually talk business that concerns my manager."

Vince sits in the chair across from me. "I'm just watching out for you. That's part of my job."

"Then let's get one thing straight—anything that has to do with Nikki doesn't involve you."

"Fine." Vince crosses his arms. "You need to come down to Vegas at least two weeks early. I have promos set. Will you be coming alone?"

"I'm not sure yet. And I only planned for a week. Why the change?"

"Because the people paying for you to fight want you there so they can hype it up more. Hype equals dollars, you know that."

Craig shoots me an expression to say Vince has got a point. But I'm not ready to leave Nikki early. We still have so many logistics to discuss. I guess tonight is the night to air them out.

"Fine, but you might as well roll up your sleeves, because I'm not leaving until this studio is done for Nikki." I stand and open the door to tell the crew to come back in and work.

For the rest of the afternoon, Vince is on his best behavior—and who would've known he can use a nail gun?

THE BEST NEWS I got all day was that Vince didn't want to

sleep at the Linville house with Nikki and me, so he's staying in Anchorage. A blissful forty-five minutes away.

After dinner, Nikki's chilling on the couch, so I sit down beside her and bring her feet to my lap. I massage them, and she closes her eyes and moans.

"Keep making sounds like that and I'll be massaging something else," I joke.

"I wouldn't complain." She peeks her eyes open and smiles at me.

"I wanted to talk to you about a few things." Her eyes open wide now. Maybe I should've started the conversation a different way. "Just hear me out before your mind goes crazy."

"Okay."

"I have to go back to Vegas two weeks before the fight. I thought it was only a week, but I was wrong. Vince told me this afternoon."

She relaxes into the couch. "You scared me for a minute." Sitting up, she kisses me on the lips. "It's okay, but I can't come until closer to the fight."

"I know and I'll send a plane for you. Does any of the rest of your family want to come?"

She shrugs. "I don't know, but I'll ask."

She shifts to go back to lying down, but I reach for her so she stays on my lap.

"Not so fast," I say. "I have one more thing to talk about."

Her head falls to my shoulder. "What?" There's a slight whine to her tone, and I doubt myself for a moment, wondering if now is the time to ask her.

"I know we're only dating."

She laughs and looks up.

"But I'd like us to discuss what's going to happen after the fight."

"Me too." she says, her gaze growing serious.

"Do I come back here? Do you stay in Vegas? Do we continue to date? Do you change your name finally?"

"That's a lot of questions."

I nod, not taking my eyes off of her. "Let's try one at a time. Do I come back?"

"I don't hold the keys to the gates of Sunrise Bay."

I push a strand of her hair behind her ear. "You know what I'm asking." My heart is in my throat as I wait for her to answer.

"I'd like you to come back here, but I understand if—"

I put my finger to her lips. "That's all the answer I need."

I replace my finger with my lips. We get carried away, and soon I'm lying over her on the couch.

"I think that made Logan Stone happy."

I draw back and stare into her eyes. "Very happy. Now we have to figure out where we're going to live and how long it will take for you to change your last name."

She laughs. "We're still dating, Mr. Stone."

"Not according to the world."

She shakes her head and rolls her eyes. "You have an answer for everything."

"That's right, I do. Oh, and I have some news for you. I solidified your first guest for your podcast."

She shoves at my chest in a playful way. "You know you don't have to do that anymore now that we're... you know.... a real couple."

I hold up my hand. "I'm a man of my word."

"That's very sweet." She opens up her legs and my hips fall between them.

"I'm a sweet husband."

"Yes, you are."

"Are you going to ask who it is?" I kiss her neck and my lips move down to her collarbone.

"Who?" she asks a little breathily.

"Gavin Price." I draw back to see her expression.

Gavin Price is an actor and a friend. He agreed to come up here and let Nikki interview him. It helps that he just got blasted in the magazines for not being easy to work with and the press is saying he's washed up. She could do the interview remotely, but he said he'd be happy to get away from Los Angeles for bit and come visit.

Her mouth falls open. "But he's so famous. He'll come up here?"

"Try not to hurt your husband's ego." I pretend I'm hurt, but I understand her feelings. Gavin is pretty famous, and luckily, he loves coming to MMA fights, which is how I met him. "Now how could you make it up to me..."

"I can think of a few ways." She unbuttons her blouse, teasing me with a glimpse of her bra. She almost has it completely open when her phone rings on the coffee table.

"Forget it," I say, my head dipping to her cleavage.

"It's Mandi, give me a second." She snatches up the phone and answers.

I don't stop my exploration of her body and she smiles, swatting me away with a giggle, but we both know she loves it.

"What?" She bolts up and I fling back across the couch. "Seriously?" She's quiet for a second. "How do you know for sure?" She gives me these wide eyes like I'm not going to believe it. "Okay, thanks for letting me know. Yeah, he's here. I'll tell him. Bye, Mandi." She hangs up and her head falls in her hands.

"What is it?" She doesn't answer, so I pry her hands away. "Nik?"

She lets me see her face, and she looks as if she might cry. What the hell happened? "Mandi said she had two people from the press check in. They were asking questions about you and me. Whether she knew me and where they might find us."

I close my eyes. Why the hell did the press wait this long to come here? And of course, just as I'm making progress with Nikki. I wish I knew for sure she'll take this okay, but I'm not sure she will.

Chapter Twenty-seven

Nikki

I should've known the press would eventually find us. We've been in this bubble for so long after our marriage that you'd think someone paid them off not to bother us. Why are they just now showing up in Sunrise Bay, and why didn't they do enough of an investigation to know that Mandi is my sister?

"Hey." Logan pries my hands away from my face. "We can handle this. We're happy and that's all they're gonna find."

"It's not us I'm worried about. It's me, my family. They're gonna be digging around."

He sits back on the couch. "Are you sure it's only your family?"

I don't need him doubting my feelings for him right now. "Yes, Log. Let's remember my mom married her husband's cousin. That can be twisted in a lot of different ways."

He looks me straight in the eye. "Your mom and Hank

are in love. They're not gonna care about that. I promise they're only here for me and you."

I blow out a breath. "The night we met, did I tell you why I wanted to start this podcast?"

This isn't the ideal time for us to delve into our deep dark pasts, but this will help Logan understand that I am only concerned about my family and not what they'll find between the two of us. If it means opening up to him, well, I have no choice, and he's more than proven I can trust him.

"So they can tell their own side of their story." He smiles at me. "It's a great idea. A lot of people just believe what they're told."

I nod. "Yeah, but the reason it's so important to me is that when my dad cheated on my mom, all these rumors started spreading. How my mom knew and turned a blind eye for years because she didn't want to give up their lifestyle. Other people said my parents were swingers and they'd host orgies. The worst rumor was that they'd pimp us out at their parties." I roll my eyes just thinking about it.

"Kids are assholes."

"That's the thing—it wasn't just the kids, it was the adults too. Once my family was torn apart, my mom had no choice but to return to Sunrise Bay because our lives were becoming a living hell down there. The people we thought were our friends turned out to be the most vicious of all."

His hand lands on my thigh. "I'm sorry you had to go through that."

I shrug. "It was a long time ago, but let's not forget that even here in Sunrise Bay, when my mom and Hank got together, not everyone was happy about it. Some kids called them kissing cousins even though they're not blood related. At least up here, people aren't so hung up on making sure they're on the top of the pedestal that they kick anyone who gets close in the face to tumble back down. It's not Arizona, but I'm concerned that all the press is gonna focus on is that you married a girl who's related to her stepdad."

He takes my hand, tugging me up from my position to straddle him. His hand molds to my ass and our eyes lock. "I'll take care of this, Nik. You're my wife, which means it's my responsibility to make sure you're safe and secure."

My forehead falls to his shoulder. "You can't be sure, and you can't control what they're going to say. They're gonna have a field day."

His hands land on either side of my cheeks, and he pulls me away from his shoulder. "I can be sure, because I won't stand for anyone making up lies. I have a platform and I'll use it if we need to, but we're in this together."

Never in my life did I think I'd fall for a man I married immediately after meeting him, but I have fallen for him. So much so that I'd take his last name and truly see where this marriage could go. He might just be one in a million.

"Trust me?" he asks.

I still for a second, then nod. He exhales, letting out a relieved breath because he understands how hard it is for me to be vulnerable and hand over my heart. Then he stands up.

I yelp as I try to hang on. "Where are we going?"

"We're going to bed," he whispers in my ear. "I want to make love to my wife."

Goose bumps travel down my spine as he carries me up to the master bedroom where the majority of my stuff has accumulated. I hold on to his neck as though I could lose him at any time. Once we're in the bedroom, he lowers me to the bed and climbs up and over me.

"Shouldn't we talk about the press?" I ask.

He puts his finger over my mouth and shakes his head.

"They'll be there tomorrow. Tonight, it's just us." He unbuttons the rest of my blouse, his palms push the fabric away from my skin. "You're so beautiful, Nik," he says with awe in his voice.

I arch, allowing his hand to mold to my breast, needing to feel him more in this moment than ever before.

Reaching back on the neckline of his T-shirt, he tears the shirt off his body. My fingers outline the tattoo on his chest. He doesn't tear his gaze away as I'm transfixed on him.

"God, Logan," I murmur.

"What?" he asks, his fingers unbuttoning my pants and sliding the zipper down.

"You. I never would have thought..." I struggle to finish my thought when he slides his hand down my pants, playing with my clit over my soaked silk panties.

He kisses the hollow of my neck. "Thought what?"

"That I'd..."

He straightens out and smirks at me. "You don't have to say it."

I shake my head. "I want to." I swallow past the dryness in my throat and lock my eyes with his. "I've fallen for you, Logan Stone, and it scares the crap out of me."

He chuckles. "Join the party, but it's all going to be okay. I promise to never break your heart."

For the next hour, we slowly touch one another, our lips exploring each other's bodies. And in that bedroom, Logan makes love to me while promising no one will ever harm me on his watch. By the time I fall asleep naked beside him, wrapped up in his arms, I've never felt safer or more loved in my entire life.

IT TOOK two days for them to dig up my parents' past. Obviously, we're not talking about the best in their profession here. All they had to do was talk to the townspeople and someone would've spilled the beans.

Logan and I are at my mom and Hank's, and I look around the group gathered in the kitchen.

"I'm sorry, guys," I say, thinking about what they have to endure because I married an MMA fighter on a whim.

"They're gonna get bored," Xavier, my stepbrother, says. He's a professional football player and the person taking the most heat since the public cares more about him than any of us. It's not that Xavier's never had press about our family before, but they didn't spin it in a negative way back when he started playing pro. "They'll move on and no one will remember this. Trust me." He squeezes my shoulder.

Logan takes my hand. "He's right. Eventually they won't find anything else they can try to spin and move on."

"Still. You're all under a microscope because of me."

"Nik, this family has weathered worse storms than this." My mom places small cucumber sandwiches on the table. All the boys reach in at once.

"I get it," Presley says on the other side of me.

I smile at her. "Thanks."

My family all seem to understand, and as a consensus, we've all decided to remain quiet and not to talk to anyone —a united front.

Everyone disperses from the table, leaving Logan and me with my mom and Hank.

"I think I should go back to Vegas early. They'll follow me there and leave you guys alone." Logan takes my hands. "You can come down closer to the fight. I have to be down there for promo soon anyway."

"But—"

He shakes his head. "It only makes sense. They're intruding here, and I imagine it will only get worse. I'll leave and they'll follow. I know it."

"Are you suggesting we're boring, Logan?" Hank asks, laughing.

"Not at all."

Hank raises his hand. "I'm fully aware I live what some might think is a boring life and I'm proud of it. I have everything I'll ever need."

He looks at my mom with that expression he has since they got together. They have a love I've always been envious of, the same love I'm sometimes certain Logan and I hold for one another. Only we're like a new bud that's just blooming and they're an entire rose garden.

Cade comes back into the kitchen to grab a drink from the fridge.

"What do you think?" Logan asks me.

"I don't want you to go early." I frown, knowing I'll miss him.

"You shouldn't have to change your life for them. I hate all these people who make a living off of poking their noses into other people's affairs." My mom grabs her iced tea, leans back in her chair, and sips it.

Cade was leaving the kitchen, but he stops and turns around when he hears what my mom says. "You mean like Nikki?"

I narrow my eyes on him. "I report the truth and you know it. And I don't put a spin on things to suit me or make it sound juicier."

He puts his hands up in front of him. "I'm just saying... it's kind of like karma got you on this one, Nik. Do you realize how much it sucks now?"

"I can handle it. But this is about my mom and Hank, who have nothing to do with my marriage."

He nods. "True enough." Then he leaves the kitchen.

"He's always hated my job," I mumble to Logan before turning to look back at him. "Anyway, like I was saying, I don't want you to go early."

"I agree with you, but as of right now, we don't have a choice. After the fight, they won't care about me or my relationships." Logan squeezes my hands. "I'll head back to Vegas and they'll leave you and your family alone."

I sulk in the chair. The thought of us trying this long distance scares me down to my bones. All my insecurities creep back in, even though I'm certain I can trust Logan. He's never shown me I can't, but then again, we haven't been together that long and he's been living here, not the lifestyle he usually does.

But then there's my family... I can't put them through this. It's tourist season, and bad rumors or outright lies could hurt all their businesses.

"Okay," I say, and my heart immediately feels as if a bulldozer rolled over it.

"It won't be long. Plus, you're kind of a distraction." He winks. I playfully shove him, and he boomerangs back, giving me a kiss on the temple. "Just kidding."

I glance over and see my mom's frown. Is she as scared as I am of what distance could do to our relationship?

Logan

On the walk back home from Nikki's parents, I debate in my head on whether or not to show her the half-finished podcast studio rather than waiting for it to be fully finished. But with me leaving town early, if I don't show her I run the risk of someone slipping and ruining the secret.

"Hey," I say, taking her hand. "I have something I want to show you before we head home."

She glances over at me with suspicion and trepidation. "Okay."

"Don't worry, it's a good thing."

She chuckles. "I'll admit you scared me a little there."

"Like I was going to give you the 'it's me, not you' speech?"

She says nothing and I'd be lying if I said I didn't like the fact that she doesn't want to break up, that she's truly in this relationship with her whole heart.

"You can't get rid of me that easily." I squeeze her hand, waiting for her to look over at me. When she does, I smile and she matches my grin, laying her head on my shoulder for a moment while we walk.

I slow my steps as we near the shop.

"Are you going to show me your moves?" She stops in front of Pump It Up, assuming that's where we're going.

I tug on her hand. "I show you my moves every night."

She laughs. "I particularly like the 'against the wall' move."

"Me too." I waggle my eyebrows, stepping up in front of the shop next door that still has brown paper covering the windows. Hank was adamant that in this town we needed to cover everything up if I didn't want Nikki to find out.

"What's this?" She tilts her head while I retrieve a key out of my pocket.

"Just wait. I wish I had a blindfold."

"Hmm... a blindfold and a building with covered windows. Now I'm scared in a whole other way."

I chuckle and use the key to open up the door. Holding it open, I flick on the light then wait for her to step into the space first. Following her, I lock the door behind us and watch her gaze scatter around the room. "What is this?"

"This will be where you record your podcast." I point to the spot by the window. "I thought it would be cool for people to walk by and see you interviewing your guests."

First she looks at me like I'm crazy but right after, her shoulders fall and her hands go to her mouth. "Logan," she says my name like she's in disbelief, which makes my chest swell with pride. And my ego a little too.

"You need a place to do your interviews." I shove my hands in my pockets, unsure what to say. "It's not quite done yet only because I have to leave town early, but I promise I'll get it finished up right after I get back from the fight."

"You did this for me?"

I nod.

She slowly walks over to me and slides her arms around my waist. "This is way too much," she whispers and buries her head into my chest.

I draw back and put my finger under her chin, urging her to look at me. The tears welling in her eyes is all the appreciation I need. "It's not. I wanted you to have this."

"But you know that I didn't need this? I would have managed."

I shake my head at her. "I know and that's exactly why I wanted to give this to you. I know you'll make your show a success. I've always believed in the adage 'begin as you mean to go on.'"

"Thank you," she murmurs into my chest, squeezing me tight.

"You're welcome."

I hold her as long as I can, already missing her, and I haven't even left the damn state yet.

There's a knock on the front door and I overhear Nikki answering it. "Hey, Pauline, come on in."

I'm upstairs, packing my bags and wishing Nikki could come with me, but she has her job at the radio station and can't give up her spot just to follow me around while I work on my career. I'd never expect her to do that.

"Are you going with him?" Nikki asks my mom.

I have no idea what my mom thinks of Nikki and me.

Ever since she showed up here, she's spent more time away from me than with me. I assumed she'd be all up in our business. While Nikki and I have gotten together with my mom a few times a week since she arrived, it feels to me like she's carved out her own life here. Which seems odd, given that she's only visiting.

"I think I might stick around here. I really enjoy your town," my mom says.

"That's great. Mandi said you've been a huge help to her."

"I need to keep busy. I used to waitress some when Logan was growing up, so I don't mind pitching in when she's busy. Come by and I'll read your tarot cards."

That's my cue to get downstairs. Who knows what those tarot cards will say, and I'm not about to put any more doubts in Nikki's head just because some card that can be interpreted different ways turns up in her shuffle.

"Hey, Mom." I drop my suitcase on the floor and catch Nikki's gaze, diverting to it for a second. Yeah, this sucks.

"You're leaving, I hear," Mom says.

I nod. "I leave and the press comes with me."

"You know, I did one of their tarot card readings the other night. I'm not sure who these people are, but they didn't even know I'm your mom. How dense is that?" She shakes her head. "I may have fibbed a little about their future outlook."

Nikki laughs. "You didn't have to do that."

"You're my daughter-in-law and they're being intolerable."

"Well, thanks." Nikki glances at me. "Craig going too?"

"Yeah, the whole training group. I need them in Vegas."

"Don't go on one of those strict diets and turn into skin

and bones. You need some fat on your body to block those punches."

"Thanks, Mom."

My mom runs her hand down Nikki's arm. "Can I have a moment with my son?"

Nikki nods. "Of course, I'll just be in the kitchen."

Once Nikki's gone and out of earshot, my mom signals for me to step farther away. "Are you sure you're making the right decision? Just leaving like this?"

"They won't bother her if I'm not here."

She raises her eyebrows. "You can't guarantee that. Plus, if she's going to be your wife, this is a part of your life. Whenever you have something going on, she'll have a camera in her face, pictures taken when she has no makeup on, and yeah, lies spread about you both. She might as well get used to it now."

I tug on my mom's sleeve to step even farther away so Nikki can't hear me. "She will get used to it, but we haven't even known one another that long. Trust takes time to build, and I'm trying to do this with baby steps to ease her into it. I'm not going to push her into the deep end of the pool and say sink or swim."

"You're protecting her."

"Yeah." I nod. "I am, and I'm not ashamed. We'll get there, but not right now. This is the best decision for us at this point."

She wraps her arms around my shoulders. "Okay, if you think so. I'll be at your fight in a few weeks then."

I understand what my mom is thinking, but things have progressed so fast for Nikki and me. If I let the press eat her up now, I might as well sign the divorce papers. "Love you."

"Love you too." She runs her hands down my back.

Craig comes to the door, the other trainers all loading their bags into the truck behind him.

"I'm going to say goodbye to Craig. I think Zoe might miss him." Mom winks. I can already see her matchmaking skills hard at work.

"Remember, Craig lives in the lower forty-eight."

"So, do you?" She raises her eyebrows, and I shake my head.

"Hey, Nik?" I call after my mom leaves.

She walks in, and I can already tell from the look in her eyes that this is going to suck.

I take her in my arms and kiss her forehead. "You'll be so busy you won't even notice."

"Um... did you miss that we're in Sunrise Bay, Alaska?"

"What did you do before me?"

She rests her chin on my chest and stares up at me. "I don't remember. It feels like a lifetime ago."

I nod. "I know how you feel. Going back to Vegas doesn't seem like a good fit anymore."

She rests her hands on my chest. "It is. It's where you make your living."

I cover her hands with mine. "So I'll see you soon, right?"

"Yeah."

"I hope you like phone sex, because it's going to be a struggle without you being an arm's length away."

She giggles. "Maybe abstinence will help your training."

I shake my head. "Nah. Overrated. Done it before. Just makes me angry."

"Which is good for the ring, right?"

"You don't want to be responsible for the death of Rinaldo, do you?"

She laughs and I wish I could record it to play it over

and over again. I'm not prepared for this separation ahead of us. "Go. We can't do a long, teary goodbye. Besides, it's not goodbye, it's see you soon."

I stare at her, trying to memorize everything about her even though I snapped a picture of her sleeping last night, wondering if I'm making the right decision. The press can twist things around, and I'm counting on Nikki not to read into things she may see or hear. Distance can do crazy things to the most well-established couples. It could be suicide to our relationship.

I lean down and capture her lips in a kiss I hope conveys all my feelings for her. She moans when I slip my tongue in her mouth, and she grips me harder, her body flush to mine. Damn, I'm going to miss her something fierce. She's the one who ends the kiss, and we take a moment to catch our breath.

"I should get going," I say with a hoarse voice.

She nods a few times fast.

"I'll call you when we land."

"Great."

"You going back home tonight? I don't want you here by yourself."

She pushes me toward the door. "You do know I was a functioning adult before you came into my life, right?"

"That's before. Now it's my job to protect you."

She smiles and shakes her head. "Well, I promise I'll be fine."

I kiss her one last time before heading down the steps with my bag. Right before I step into the truck, I stare at her in the doorway. My mom's with her now, her arm through Nikki's. I can't imagine how those men who go off to war handle this because my heart is shredding from thinking about spending the next few weeks without her.

I wave and she waves back. Then I head into the truck, under the darkness of the tinted windows.

"You'd think you just broke up. It's only a few weeks." Craig slaps me on the knee.

"I'm fine," I choke out, staring at her through the window.

"Man, she sure won you over fast. I've never seen a man fall so fast and so hard." Craig laughs.

I refrain from making a crack about Zoe.

WHEN WE ARRIVE at the Anchorage airport, Vince is already in the private jet. He does love to fly on my dime. The latest gossip magazine is on the table, and I pick it up and ask the flight attendant to throw it away.

"You should know what they're saying," Vince says.

"I don't care what they're saying." I sit in my seat and strap in, as does Craig and all the other trainers.

"Being blind to the issue isn't going to make it any better."

"What issue is that?" I spear him with a look.

I've always loved Vince. He's a great manager, always has my needs in mind, but after our confrontation about Nikki, I sense his displeasure with me finding someone to share my life with. And if he doesn't want me happy in all aspects of my life, then I don't really care for him to be in my life. Which brings the thought of retirement back up. One thing I do know is that I won't retire unless I'm on top, so if I don't win this fight, I'll be going for the title again.

"The fact that you've never won a fight when you've been in a relationship."

I roll my eyes. "You know that's just a coincidence."

"Still. Every time you're in a serious relationship, you lose. Case in point, it's clear to me since I arrived in that nothing of a town that your focus is split. I hope you can turn it around once we're in Vegas and there aren't distractions."

"Watch yourself, Vince." I shoot him a warning glare, and he looks away.

He's not normally so vocal about his concerns with me. Then I remember a headline about Dale Campbell signing with someone else. Vince's eggs are still all in my basket.

Before takeoff, I send one last text

I miss you already. 😞

Three dots appear immediately.

I miss you more. 🤍

I shut the shade, not wanting to see the mountains disappear and turn into desert, and put in my earbuds. My head falls back to my headrest and all I envision is my wife spread out naked on the bed for me. I'm going to have the bluest balls ever by the time she meets me in Vegas. I need to channel all that sexual energy somewhere else, so I pull up Rinaldo's last fight to study his moves some more and figure out how I'm going to counter them.

I hate it, but Vince is somewhat right—having a wife is a distraction. A welcome distraction, but still, I'm thinking of our relationship a lot, and not one-hundred percent focused on the fight mentally like I normally would be.

Vince puts his tablet up in my face to show me an article that's just been posted.

Place your bets now... rumor has it, Logan Stone and his new bride have separated already. Finally, all those who believe in the superstition that he's never won a fight while having a girlfriend can rest assured he's moving up in the odds in Vegas now that he's single again.

I roll my eyes. Who would report we broke up? Then I shake my head, not really giving a fuck because they're wrong. If someone didn't bet on me because of that stupid superstition, screw them.

Chapter Twenty-nine

Nikki

My heart drops out of my chest when I see the article that says Logan and I broke up. It's fake news. Just like Logan explained when we talked last night, some people will do anything to gain success or money. He's been gone for a few days now, and I've been trying to keep myself busy with work and preparing for my podcast with Gavin Price, but none of it helps. I'm still always thinking of Logan in the back of my mind.

Since we're very much still together, it isn't the reported breakup that concerns me. It's the fact he's never won a fight while he's been in a relationship. So I'll be the reason if he loses? At least as far as the world is concerned? Why didn't he ever tell me that before?

"I think you're overreacting," Mandi says, sliding into the seat across from me at her restaurant attached to her inn. "You'll prove them wrong when you show up at the fight."

"I told you to poison their food while they were here," Chevelle says, crossing her arms and giving Mandi a glare.

"And murder someone?"

"I simply suggested a little digestive trouble. They deserve it for coming here and ambushing Nikki and Logan."

I close my screen, unable to read it again. The tidbit about him never winning while in a relationship took me down a Google blackhole of Logan's exes, only to find one I recognize. Melanie from the casino. She's one of the girls who holds the numbers and struts around the cage. How fucking unoriginal is that? From what I gather, they were involved for at least six months, maybe a year, and he lost every fight during that time. After they broke up, he won again and has been on a winning streak ever since.

"I can't afford a bad Yelp review," Mandi continues to argue about something I don't care about. I'm only half paying attention.

"Oh, screw Yelp. Do you know I got a review that said I was wearing too many clothes on the boat?" Chevelle rolls her eyes and flicks her long blonde hair behind her shoulder.

"Shut up?" Posey's mouth hangs open.

Chevelle nods. "There was this group of guys and they were rowdy and really annoying and probably a little embarrassed that not one of them could catch a fish. When we docked, one of them grabbed my ass."

"And what did you do?" Mandi asks.

"I was about to throw him in the water, but Cam saw and took care of it." She shrugs.

Oh, Cam. When will that guy ever admit to wanting my stepsister? He's been Fisher's best friend forever, and though Cam and Chevelle argue like siblings, I still think there's an undercurrent of desire too.

"Then I yelled at him because I can fight my own battles. I certainly don't need Cam to do it for me."

"What did Cam say?" Posey is clearly enthralled with the story. Must come with being a hairdresser. She gets gossip on the regular—not that she shares any with me for my show. She says it would be bad for business.

"He said Fisher would kick his ass if he knew he saw what happened and didn't do anything. So now I have a one-star review. Yelp took down the remark about the clothes but kept the star there. I fucking hate Yelp." Chevelle picks up a fry and dips it into her ranch dressing before popping it in her mouth. "Anyway, this is about Nikki. Carry on."

I hold up my hand. There's nothing more I can say. "I'm done. I should just go drink my sorrows away."

"Where is my sister and who stole her pussy?" Posey asks, shocking all of us. We just stare at her for a minute. "You know how people say who took your balls for a man?"

The three of us nod.

"Gotcha," I say.

"You don't believe any of that. Logan's a great guy, and he's the one who came here looking for you. Remember that," Posey says.

Posey has a point. I need to keep reminding myself of that fact if we're going to get through these weeks without one another. It might still be early days for us, but I need to believe in what Logan and I share.

"What did Dad say when you talked to him?" Mandi asks. She's the peacekeeper in our family, so she's the one who talks to Dad more than any of us.

"He wanted tickets to the fight. Which reminds me..." I pull out my phone and send Logan my dad's phone number for him to pass on to Vince to arrange the tickets. This way I don't have to be involved in any of it.

Logan doesn't respond right away, and I sigh. That's been the norm since he returned to Vegas. Even our nightly conversations often consist of him dozing off from being so tired. Last night, I told him I had to do more research on Gavin Price so he could just go to bed and wouldn't feel bad about not having a lengthy conversation with me.

"Let's go out and do something fun!" Posey says.

"I prefer to wallow," I say.

Chevelle throws a fry at me. "Posey's right. We need to get you out. The press has all left since they think you're broken up, so we're free to do what we want."

"I have to work." Mandi slides out from the table to greet a few guests.

"I need to put some more work into the podcast. I bet Molly will go with you."

Chevelle pulls out her phone and starts texting. "You're honestly a bore, Nik."

I stick out my tongue and we both laugh.

"Holy shit!" Posey says, eyeing the door. I move to turn my head, but she grabs my arm. "No."

"What is it?"

"Gavin Price is here," Posey says.

Chevelle's head flings up in the air. "*The* Gavin Price?"

I turn around, and sure enough, it is him and he's talking with Mandi.

Gavin Price is a famous child star. He was the meain character in the most popular teen drama while Posey and Chevelle were growing up, which is why their jaws are hanging open right now.

"He's gotten so manly looking," Posey says.

"He's even better looking than before," Chevelle chimes in.

He walks over to our table with Mandi and my two sisters stare but say nothing.

I put out my hand. "Hey, Gavin, I'm Nikki Greene. I think you know my husband, Logan?" Jeez, it feels weird to refer to Logan that way out loud.

Mandi brings a chair over for Gavin to join us, while whispers commence about who he is from the other people in the restaurant.

"Hey, Nikki. Good to meet you. Well, he talked to me about your podcast, but he couldn't stop raving about this town, so I felt compelled to come up and see what I'm missing. Plus, I had to get out of LA for a while."

"Coffee? Tea?" Mandi asks.

"Coffee, black. Thanks." He smiles at Mandi.

Her eyes go wide in dramatic fashion when she steps away from the table, putting her hand over her heart as if she's going to pass out. Clearly, I'm the only Greene who will manage a conversation with the man.

"You came up just to visit?" I ask.

"Yep, and I have to say, I get why Stone loves it so much."

My phone rings and I glance down to see that it's Logan. "Speaking of the man." I answer the phone. "Hello."

"What are you wearing? If the answer is clothes, I need you to rectify that immediately and send me a picture."

I giggle, thankful I didn't put him on speaker. "Funny thing..."

"Did you not hear me?" He sounds breathless. I assume he just finished a workout.

"I did, but that will have to wait."

"He's probably asking her for a nude pic," Gavin says to Posey and Chevelle, who still haven't found their voices yet.

"Gavin Price is here," I say.

There's silence on the other end of the line for a beat. "Already? He didn't let me know he was coming so soon." Logan asks in a tone I swear holds some jealousy, but why would he be jealous of a man I just met?

"He said you raved about the town, so he wanted to come up and visit."

"But the podcast isn't happening yet. You're not ready," he says in an almost panicked tone I don't understand.

"I know. Do you want to talk to him?"

Gavin holds out his hand and I pass the phone before Logan's even agreed.

"How's Vegas?" Gavin asks and listens. "You worked out in a sweaty gym for the last four hours while I get to sit at a table full of beautiful women. One of us got the shit end of the stick, Stone, and it wasn't me." He laughs.

I kick Chevelle and Posey under the table and they both straighten in their chairs, scowling at me. Hopefully that knocks them out of their trance.

Gavin talks to Logan for a few minutes then hands me back the phone. "He wants his wife."

I stand and leave the table. God willing, Mandi can run interference between him and my newly mute sisters. "Was that jealousy I heard in your voice?" I take a seat in the small lobby of the inn.

"Damn right it was. I know all the women think Price is gorgeous, and now he gets to be there with you."

"I never watched his show, if that makes you feel better."

He chuckles. "God, this is pure torture."

"It's not too much longer."

"I know, but it's not ending soon enough. I wish you could come down this weekend."

"I can't. Remember we broke up?"

He laughs. "Don't keep telling yourself that. Otherwise, you'll start to believe it."

"Never," I say.

He blows out a long breath. The man has done everything he can to make sure I know he's thinking of me all the time and I need to start repaying him.

"You sound frustrated." I say.

"Hell yeah. You know that right before the fight, I'm going to fuck you every which way I can think of."

"Are you sure you shouldn't wait until after the fight?"

"Not an option." There's finality in his tone.

I debate for a moment, then tell Logan to hold on for a minute. I sneak into the bathroom and lock myself in a stall. Tearing off my shirt, I unhook my bra and snap a selfie, then I send it to Logan.

"Crap, hold on, someone texted me... fuck... you're so damn sexy." He comes back on the line and I hear some wrestling like he's situated himself. "Don't mind me beating off to you right now. Wanna talk dirty to me?"

"Tell me what you're doing with your hand," I say, putting my bra and T-shirt back on. I don't have the freedom, in a public bathroom, to do what he is.

"I'm fisting myself right now, pumping slowly and staring at your delicious tits that I'm going to be motorboating next time I see you."

"I look forward to it." No man has ever made me feel more wanton than Logan.

"Shit, your skin looks so smooth and silky. I imagine my hands running around your waist and my fingers pinching your nipples, how your back arches as though you're offering them to me. Now my mouth is on them. I'm nibbling on your nipples and your fingers are tugging on my hair because you want me to stay there."

I close my eyes and lean back against the stall door, imagining the scene unfolding. "I take you into my palm, squeezing your hard cock and pumping you up and down. My thumb runs your precum around the tip and then I fall to my knees. You groan and turn my head so I'm looking at you while I open my mouth and push you inside. I swirl my tongue over your tip, and you buck into my mouth."

"Fuck, Nikki, don't stop," he says like he's on the edge.

"I bring you all the way to the back of my throat and you reach down, grabbing a hold of my tits, pushing them together, and pinching my nipples. God, it feels good, and soon I take my hands off you, putting them on your ass to drive you in and out of my hot, wet mouth. Oh fuck, Log." I pant, my hand diving into my pants and sliding under my panties.

"Now I'm going to fuck you so hard you're gonna black out."

I close my eyes tighter, and my body goes rigid, waiting for the release.

"My dick slides between your folds and damn, you're soaked from wanting me."

"I'm so wet," I say.

"Hmm... next time send a picture of that." He doesn't pause for long. "My dick slides into you and you sigh from the satisfaction."

"Faster," I say.

"I'm going faster. I shift onto my back and you take control, straddling me, and position the tip of my cock at your entrance. Then you're riding me and I'm grabbing your tits. You're screaming, I'm shouting, skin is smacking."

"Don't stop," I tell him.

"I'm driving in and out so hard, then I put my finger on

your clit and I run circles around it. Come on, baby, come for me," he says, and I do.

"Nikki, you in here?" someone calls out.

My phone falls out of my hand—right into the toilet.

Damn it. I hope he finished before I dropped the phone. Fingers crossed that Mandi has some rice in her kitchen I can throw my phone in, otherwise I'll have to make a run into Greywall tomorrow to get a new one.

I pull my phone out of the toilet and leave the stall to find Ethel standing there with her hands on her hips. "Your cheeks are flushed, dear, are you feeling okay?"

I nod, washing my hands. "I'm great. Just overwhelmed."

Hopefully it's been so long that Ethel forgets what a postorgasmic glow looks like.

Chapter Thirty

Logan

It's been two weeks since I saw Nikki face to face, and Craig says I'm becoming a real asshat. Nikki and I have tried it all. Phone sex, video sex, dirty texts, but none of it is as satisfying as when I have her in my arms and on my dick. With one week to go, I couldn't be happier that I'll be able to see her soon.

Since tonight I have a promo event, the night will probably suck more than usual. Lately, I've resorted to going to bed early just to pass the time.

Vince calls me from downstairs, so I exit the suite and take the elevator through the back entrance to hop into the black SUV. He's on the phone and his leg is bouncing a mile a minute. Great. Something has him riled up.

Once he's off the phone, I ask, "What's up?"

"Nothing. It's just people are asking what you're going to do. Since you haven't told me, I'm unsure how to answer."

I narrow my eyes. "What the hell are you talking about?"

"About your possible retirement. They want to know before the fight so they can really push it."

"Who?"

"The casino, the organizers, your sponsors."

"I told you I won't go out without being the champion. There's no way I'm announcing it beforehand." I stare out the window as we drive down the Strip. Lately, I've felt as though Vince wants me to retire, but I don't understand why. He has no one to fill my shoes and the man doesn't understand the concept of saving money.

"Relax, I told them you have no plans of leaving the sport."

"Good."

We continue the ride in silence. I don't think I'm imagining that I used to feel as though Vince was a friend and had my best interests at heart, that he was my protector. But something about him isn't sitting well in my gut ever since Nikki entered my life. I've been trying to ignore it, but it keeps creeping back up. The coincidence of him showing up in Alaska, then the press a day later. His angry outburst at me for staying married to her. If he really cared for me, he'd be happy I found happiness with her, right?

I shake my head, not wanting to go down that rabbit hole right now. I want to focus on tonight. Other fighters will be there, so at least I can socialize with them.

When the SUV pulls up to the red carpet event my sponsor is hosting, I wait for the driver to open my door before I walk up to the roped area, signing autographs and taking pictures. Vince is nowhere in sight by the time I reach the lobby.

"Log!" a woman calling my name makes me turn around and I see Melanie.

I inwardly groan. The woman doesn't have a clue. "Hey, Mel."

She's dressed in a short red sequin dress that hides none of her body. She sticks out her tits when I acknowledge her, though I'm not checking her out. Actually, all I was thinking about was what Nikki would wear at a thing like this. I know my woman would choose something sexy and classy at the same time.

Melanie leans forward and presses her tits up against my chest, her lips reaching my cheek. I step back.

"I heard you're single now?"

"Don't believe everything you read." I hold up my left hand. "I'm very much a happily married man."

"Logan," someone says, and I look over to see a flash. After I blink and recover, I see Melanie's pressed next to me, smiling.

I shake my head. "Stop."

"What? They wanted a picture for old times' sake."

"Are you playing some sort of game?"

Melanie and I didn't work out because she was with me for the money. At first maybe it was me, but soon she was asking to go on shopping trips, leaving hints of expensive stuff she wanted, and making it known she was ready to give up her job and travel with me. I was all for the travel, but I want a woman with goals and dreams.

In order for a relationship to go the distance, I think both parties need their own passions. Which is why as much as these weeks without Nikki have sucked, I think they're good for us.

"No game. I just miss you. And since your wife can't be bothered to come to this, I thought you might want some company."

I remove Melanie's hand from my arm. "She's working. That's why she's not here. Excuse me."

"You're going to grow tired of small-town life. I'm sure her idea of crazy sex is having the lights on."

I stuff my hands in my pockets before I flip her off, and I walk away, fully aware that I'll have to explain that picture before Nikki sees it.

THE NEXT MORNING, I call Nikki and she answers on the first ring. "Hey you," she says with a smile in her voice.

"I wanted to let you know, Vince talked to your dad and the tickets are set."

"Oh, thank you so much for handling that for me. I was just having a great dream about us."

"I wish I had time for you to tell me about it, but I have a press event I have to get ready for."

She groans. "I have no idea how you handle all this press stuff and answering the same questions over and over again. Wish I could help you though. You sound stressed."

"You'll be here early afternoon tomorrow, so just make sure you're ready to be ravished." I laugh, and she does too.

"I can't wait."

"Me either."

I tap the pen against the paper on the nightstand and take a deep breath to try to calm my racing nerves. "There's something I need to talk to you about, something you might see online from last night."

She's silent and my stomach sours that I'm about to ruin her day.

After what feels like a lifetime, she asks, "What?"

"Melanie ambushed me at the party, and someone took our picture."

"Oh."

"Please just hear me out. It was all of a sudden. She came to say hello, and I was just dismissing her when she pressed herself against me and someone took a picture."

"Logan," she says.

"I mean, she just got in close to make it appear like we were a couple."

"Logan."

"I told her to get off me. That I was a happily married man."

She laughs. "Logan."

"What?"

"It's okay. I understand. You're going to have your picture taken with a lot of people."

"But she's my ex," I say.

"I know. It's okay. I trust you."

I want to ask her to repeat that last sentence. "Really?"

She chuckles. "Jeez, I know I'm sensitive, but a picture isn't going to set me off."

I nod, although she can't see me. "Oh, great."

"You really do need sex. You're so high strung."

"Remember that when you arrive tomorrow. I'll call you tonight before I go to bed."

"Hey, Logan?" she says before I have a chance to hang up.

"Yeah?"

"Thank you for telling me. I appreciate that you didn't keep me in the dark until after I saw it."

I blow out a breath. "I want this to work. I'll always be upfront with you."

"You're something else."

"Nah, I'm just your husband."

She's quiet for a moment. "See you tomorrow."

"I'm counting the hours."

We both hang up and I sit there for a moment, rehashing the conversation. Maybe distance is what we needed to really find that trust between us. I'll be honest, I'm surprised at how cool Nikki played it when I told her. Surprised, but happy.

A knock on my door says it's time to go, so I rise up off the bed and head out to do my job, feeling more optimistic than I ever have about our future.

Chapter Thirty-one

Logan

I'm in the elevator, waiting impatiently for the car to reach my floor so I can grab my phone from my room. I'm supposed to be having a massage right now, but once I reached the spa, I realized I forgot my phone. Nikki's supposed to be here already, but there was some issue with the plane. I don't want to be out of touch if she needs me. I wish the damn elevator would hurry up. I'm gonna be late for this appointment.

The elevator dings and the doors open on my floor. To my shock, I find my wife standing there.

"Nik!" I open my arms and step inside. Our lips meet and the weeks spent apart fade away with my wife back in my arms. "Vince told me you weren't coming for another two hours. He said something happened with the plane."

"What? I texted you when we took off."

My forehead wrinkles. "I never got a text." I remember checking my phone when Vince and I were grabbing something to eat before I headed up to the buffet.

She pulls out her phone, and sure enough, there's a text she sent to my number.

"Weird. But come on, forget my massage. I'll work off this tension with you." I kiss her again. When the elevator reaches the level my suite is on, I take her bag and grab her hand, tugging her down the hall.

"You were going for a massage?" she asks and her voice stutters.

I glance over my shoulder since she's no longer walking with me. "Not anymore, but yeah, Vince set it up since you were going to be coming in late. But I forgot my phone, so I was just headed back up to get it in case you called."

"He made the appointment for you?" she asks. Something in her voice seems off.

"Yeah, but all they care about is I pay, so come on, we're wasting valuable time." I insert my key card into the lock and the green light flashes. "You're still clothed. We made a deal, remember?"

"Logan," she says and stares at me, not moving.

"What's wrong?"

Tears fill her eyes and quickly pile up on one another, cascading down her face. "I was just in your room. That's why I was leaving..."

I keep the door open with my toe and pull her toward me. She doesn't wrap her arms around my waist but stands there with her tears wetting my T-shirt. "What am I missing?"

The door opens up all the way behind me, and I stumble back a step.

"There you are, babe." Melanie stands in the doorway. "Sorry, I couldn't get out of here soon enough before she showed up."

I'm in shock for a second, my mouth hanging open before I look at Nikki and use my finger to push her chin up to look me in the eye. "Is this why you're crying?"

She nods and all I see is red.

Releasing Nikki, I storm inside my suite. "What the fuck is going on?"

Stalking into my bedroom, I find Melanie's suitcase and her shit strewn around the room. I pick up clothes and throw them into her case.

"What are you doing, babe? It's okay, just tell her. She already knows." Melanie's voice sounds behind me, and I clench my fists to rein in my temper.

Nikki stands by the door, wiping her tears. "Did you set this whole thing up alone?" she asks Melanie.

"I'm not telling you anything. It wasn't a setup." Then she turns to me. "Logan, you can't keep her in the dark forever. Just tell her."

"There's nothing to tell." I throw Melanie's bag out of the suite, then I take her hand and lead her into the hallway. "Have a nice life and stop fucking with mine."

I slam the penthouse door and flip the lock. My anger is so all-consuming, I clench my fists at my sides and scream so that I don't put a fist through a wall. Nikki startles but doesn't move, so I rush over to her.

"You have to know that was her playing some kind of game."

She nods.

"Really? You believe me?"

She looks at me, chewing the inside of her cheek. "I did at first, but when I saw all her stuff here in the suite, I can't lie... it looked incriminating."

Fuck Melanie for ruining my reunion with Nikki.

"You're crying because you thought I cheated on you?"

She shakes her head.

Thank god, because I was about to go ballistic.

"I'm crying because for a moment, I doubted you. It was so small, but there was still a moment. What if I never fully trust you?"

My head falls back, and I sigh. I should be deep inside her by now, not reassuring her of my feelings and my faithfulness. "With what she did, Nikki, anyone would've thought that."

"But what if, Logan? What if these fears of mine never go away?" She sits on the couch and buries her head in her hands. "What if I'm just always screwed up? You live a lifestyle that scares me."

I sit and rest my forearms on my legs and link my hands together. "I can't say it doesn't hurt that you thought for even a moment that I'd screw around on you, but I can't blame you. Someone went to a great deal of trouble to create an elaborate plan to convince you."

"Logan," she whispers. "I don't think it was only Melanie."

I nod because I agree with her. I don't think it was either. "Vince?"

"He told me you were up here and had planned a surprise for me, and that's why you weren't downstairs. He was there to give me the key."

"And he came to Sunrise Bay and then suddenly so did the press." I go to the windows, wishing I could punch the shit out of one of them. I shake my head. "I need to go find him. I'll meet you at the press event."

"Do you want me to go with you?" She stands.

I shake my head.

"Is this about us?" she asks. "I know I should've believed you one-hundred percent. It was only a second, Logan."

I hold up my hand. "Craig will get a hold of you."

"But—"

"Please, Nikki, just meet me there."

I walk out of the hotel suite and shut the door. Before hopping in the elevator, I message Craig to ask him to get Nikki and her family to the press event on time.

Up until this point, I didn't know what I'd decide to do after this fight. But now, after the stunt Vince just pulled, my decision is made and final. I hate that Nikki thinks I'm mad, because I'm not, but if I tell her what I'm thinking, she'll try to talk me out of it. I'll need to help her understand this is for me and our future.

The elevator stops on the ground floor and I walk out of the hotel, onto the Strip, to clear my head for a while, wondering if I have the guts to pull this off.

Nikki's not in my room when I go up to change, which means Craig has already escorted them to the event room. The room smells like her perfume, which stirs my dick. But there will be plenty of time for that later.

After changing into my suit, I head downstairs to the press event and find Craig behind the scenes.

"What the hell is going on?" he asks.

I look around and pull him into one of the empty rooms. "Where's Vince?"

"Where's Vince? Man, who cares? Nikki looks like she lost her dog. Are you guys okay?"

"I need to know where Vince is."

Craig looks confused, but he says, "He's in the press room, making sure everything is set for the weigh-in."

I shut the door of the room. "I'm retiring."

His shoulders sink, but he nods. "I figured as much. Retiring to enjoy the good life, huh?"

I laugh. "Yeah. I've had my fun, made my money, and now it's time for me to live a quiet life with a wife and hopefully some kids."

He claps me on the shoulder. "I'm proud of you."

"I'll try to hook you up with someone else. You're way too talented to not be on a team."

"It's okay, I'm getting old too."

"Who you calling old?" I pretend to jab him in the stomach.

A knock on the door says it's time, and a queasiness fills my stomach. I should be relaxed right now, ready to go out there and play up my rivalry with my opponent to up the anticipation for the fans. But I know what I'm about to go out there and do, and even though I'm a hundred percent sure of my decision, it's a big step.

Craig and I walk out and up on the stage. Nikki and her family are pressed against the wall at the back, the reporters taking up the first few rows of seats.

Vince is already there, smiling at me, and when I sit down, he covers the mic and leans in. "Sorry about Melanie. I don't know how she got up there. I already apologized to Nikki. Never again."

I nod and try not to give away that I know he was involved.

The president of the league gets up on the microphone and introduces me. A few reporters try to ask me questions, but I raise my hand to stop them.

"I only have one announcement to make." I look at Vince. "Actually, two."

The room quiets down.

"I'll be retiring after tomorrow's fight," I say.

Vince's mouth hangs open, but he recovers quickly, putting his hand over my microphone. "You don't mean that. We need to discuss this."

I remove his hand and stare at him as I say, "And Vince is no longer my manager. You're fired."

I'm about to stand and leave when Nikki screams, "No! He's not retiring."

"Nik," I say.

She hands her purse to Molly and walks toward the front along the side wall. "I'm not letting you retire."

"It's not your decision." She joins me on the platform, and I stand and place my hands on her hips. "I want a life. A life with you, my wife. Where we go to duo nights, and sit on the porch, and watch movies and... what do you people do in the winter?"

"Make babies!" Ethel screams.

I look toward the back of the room and laugh before turning my attention back to Nikki. "Make babies. Lots and lots of babies."

She shakes her head, tears building in her eyes once again. "You can't give this up just because I'm messed up in the head."

I laugh. "You're not messed up in the head. This lifestyle plays games with the best of people and I'm done with it. I've accomplished what I set out to do. You mean more to me than any of it."

"Are you sure?" she asks.

"I'm positive. Your mood swings are enough of an adrenaline rush."

She playfully swats at me, but I take her in my arms and kiss her cheek.

"Wherever you are is where I want to be," I whisper.

She pulls back from our embrace and holds my upper arms. "Then go beat the shit out of Brett Rinaldo tomorrow night."

"Consider it done." I kiss her while everyone in the back of the room cheers. They're not the only cheers I've got in my life, but they're the best.

Epilogue

Nikki

A little less than a year later...

The boys have decided to hold fight nights at their house, and since we couldn't all get together last night, we're here on a Sunday afternoon, watching the recording. A part of me wonders if it's hard for Logan to attend these nights, but he insists he enjoys himself. He did, in fact, retire a champion—although tonight, someone else earned that belt since he doesn't get to keep it forever because he retired.

"Do you still not believe me?" Logan puts his arm around me while we watch the new champion hold up his belt. "Look at Rinaldo's face. I was able to keep mine all pretty." He pats his cheek and smiles.

I will say the fight a year ago between him and Rinaldo was brutal to watch. Although I found myself standing and cheering him on, the nursing him back to health part was hard for me. Seeing my strong husband barely able to get up off the couch was tough. They both fought an incredible fight, and Rinaldo is now the belt winner. But only because he doesn't have to compete against my husband.

I pat his cheek. "I do love seeing you without any bruises and cuts."

Logan bought Pump It Up and turned one half of it into a boxing gym and left the other half as is. Who would've thought we needed one of those in Sunrise Bay? But business has been good. Plus, it's right next to the podcast studio he built for me.

"And I love seeing you pregnant." He places his hand on my small but growing belly as he so often does these days.

I smile and lean in to kiss him again. Shortly after returning to Sunrise Bay, we decided to start trying for a baby. We both want the same thing, so there seemed to be no point in putting it off. Besides, that's not really our style anyway. We tend to jump right in.

I'm five months pregnant and next week is our gender reveal party. I cannot wait to find out whether we're having a boy or a girl. I don't have a preference either way, but I'm just excited to get everything together for his or her arrival.

"Maybe I'll have to get Rinaldo up here for an interview. See if those baby mama rumors are true." I grin.

Logan raises his eyebrows. "Nah, I'm the only MMA fighter in your world."

I laugh and he pulls me toward him, kissing my neck. The podcast has been a great side gig for me, and I'm starting to get bigger sponsors for the show.

"Let's go home," he whispers in my ear.

We've bought a place together, closer to Adam and Lucy on the other side of the bay but right on the water. Pauline has stayed in town too, but she's renting a small one-bedroom in the downtown area by the inn so she can do her nightly tarot card readings.

"Not yet. Mom said she's coming by with a big announcement," I say.

"If she's pregnant, I'm moving in with one of you." Rylan picks up the controller since the guys are going to play video games now that the fight is done.

"She can't be pregnant," I say.

"Those two are worse than you and Logan," Xavier says. "Like right now." He signals to where I'm sitting on Logan's lap.

"Hey, seating is limited. We're doing you all a favor by sharing," Logan says.

"They'll be saying they have to go soon," Mandi says, and I stick my tongue out at her.

The door opens and my mom and Hank come inside holding flags and signs that say, "Vote Greene." We all stare as they walk around and pass them out.

Then my mom pulls out a bag of pins. "Guess what?"

"Dad's running for mayor?" Adam says.

Sam Klein, Sunrise Bay's mayor, is retiring after his term. Please tell me someone from this family isn't trying to take his place.

Hank shakes his head and puts up his hands. "Not me."

No. No. Tell me this is not happening.

"Marla is!" Hank raises his hand and she high fives him.

"That's right. I've decided to run for mayor." My mom beams.

"Why?" Mandi stares at her flag with distaste. "Don't you have enough to do?"

"You don't look happy." Mom's smile fades as she looks around the room. "None of you do."

Hank gives us all "the look." The one that says, "Make your mom happy or I'll make your life miserable."

We all force smiles.

"Awesome," Jed says. "We'll hang a sign in the brewery."

"I can put one up at Fringe," Posey pipes up. "What else do you need help with? I could be your campaign manager. Or you could run your office out of Fringe."

"Suck-up," Fisher coughs out.

Posey's not a suck-up, she just always wants to make Mom happy. But if she wants to be Mom's campaign manager, I say have at it. Better her than me.

"You'll all play a part in getting your mom elected, so put your thinking caps on," Hank says.

"As though my life wasn't embarrassing enough." Rylan groans and sinks farther into the couch. Poor kid.

Jed ruffles Rylan's hair. "Hey, maybe this will earn you points with the girls."

We all know it won't.

Another knock sounds on the door, and we look around to see who it could be. Most of us are here and accounted for. Fisher gets up and opens the door to find a man dressed in a suit.

"Did someone die?" Rylan asks mom.

She stands and so does Hank, walking toward the door.

"I'm looking for Jed Greene," the man says.

Mom, Hank, and Fisher turn around and glare at Jed. He stays on the couch, playing his video game.

"Jed," Mom says.

He looks up.

"This man is here to see you."

Jed drops the controller and walks across the room.

Lucy, Chevelle, and Cam come into the room from the kitchen to see what's happening.

"I'm Jed," he says.

"Would you like to talk outside?" the man asks, gesturing to the door.

Jed looks back at us and laughs. "Nah, I've got nothing to hide." He shrugs.

"We mailed you a letter and tried to call the number we had listed for you, but since this is a time-sensitive matter, I agreed to come out here personally. I was a friend of my client."

"Time sensitive?" Jed's forehead creases and he crosses his arms, widening his stance.

"You didn't open your mail?" Mom scolds. It's one of her biggest pet peeves.

We all look at the boys' bin of unopened mail on the table near the front door. Is anyone surprised? I don't think so.

"I've been busy," Jed says to Mom.

"My name is David Webb. I'm the lawyer and a friend of Tanya Eaton."

Jed shakes his head. "Okay..."

"Do you remember Tanya Eaton?" Mr. Webb asks.

"Oh, the day has finally arrived," Mandi says, and Mom shoots her a look to be quiet.

"What are you talking about?" I whisper to Mandi.

But the lawyer beats Mandi to the punch.

"Unfortunately, Miss Eaton passed a few weeks ago from a severe asthma attack."

"Oh," Mom sighs and puts her hand over her heart.

"I'm sorry to hear that, but I don't know a Tanya Eaton." Jed gives Mom his innocent look.

"About four years ago, you and Miss Eaton had... relations."

Leave it to my siblings to laugh about that word. Mom and Hank shush everyone.

"Those relations resulted in the conception of a little girl. Tan—Miss Eaton—has named you as the little girl's father, and according to her will, she wants you to have sole custody. She has no other living relatives."

"What?" Jed whispers, his arms dropping to his sides.

The rest of us look at one another in disbelief. Everyone but Mandi, who apparently thought this day would come.

"But first you need to come down to Minnesota and take a paternity test."

"This can't be right. I don't know this woman." Jed shakes his head.

"Here." Mr. Webb digs into his pocket and pulls out a picture. "This is Tanya and... the little girl."

We all rush to look over Jed's shoulders at the picture, and there's no denying those are Jed's hazel eyes staring back at us.

The End

ALSO BY PIPER RAYNE

The Baileys

Lessons from a One-Night Stand (FREE)

Advice from a Jilted Bride

Birth of a Baby Daddy

Operation Bailey Wedding (Novella)

Falling for My Brother's Best Friend

Demise of a Self-Centered Playboy

Confessions of a Naughty Nanny

Operation Bailey Babies (Novella)

Secrets of the World's Worst Matchmaker

Winning my Best Friend's Girl

Rules for Dating Your Ex

Operation Bailey Birthday (Novella)

The Greene Family

My Twist of Fortune (Free Prequel)

My Beautiful Neighbor (FREE)

My Almost Ex

My Vegas Groom

A Greene Family Summer Bash (Novella)

My Sister's Flirty Friend

My Unexpected Surprise

My Famous Frenemy

A Greene Family Vacation (Novella)

My Scorned Best Friend

My Fake Fiancé

My Brother's Forbidden Friend

A Greene Family Christmas (Novella)

Lake Starlight

The Problem with Second Chances

The Issue with Bad Boy Roommates

The Trouble with Runaway Brides

The Drawback of Single Dads

Plain Daisy Ranch

One Last Summer

The One I Left Behind

The One I Stood Beside

The One I Didn't See Coming

Modern Love

Charmed by the Bartender

Hooked by the Boxer

Mad about the Banker

Single Dads Club

Real Deal

Dirty Talker

Sexy Beast

Hollywood Hearts

Mister Mom

Animal Attraction

Domestic Bliss

Bedroom Games

Cold as Ice

On Thin Ice

Break the Ice

Chicago Law

Smitten with the Best Man

Tempted by my Ex-Husband

Seduced by my Ex's Divorce Attorney

Blue Collar Brothers

Flirting with Fire

Crushing on the Cop

Engaged to the EMT

White Collar Brothers

Sexy Filthy Boss

Dirty Flirty Enemy

Wild Steamy Hook-up

The Rooftop Crew

My Bestie's Ex

A Royal Mistake

The Rival Roomies

Our Star-Crossed Kiss

The Do-Over

A Co-Workers Crush

Hockey Hotties

Countdown to a Kiss (Free Prequel)

My Lucky #13 (FREE)

The Trouble with #9

Faking it with #41

Tropical Hat Trick (Novella)

Sneaking around with #34

Second Shot with #76

Offside with #55

Kingsmen Football Stars

False Start (Free Prequel)

You Had Your Chance, Lee Burrows

You Can't Kiss the Nanny, Brady Banks

Over My Brother's Dead Body, Chase Andrews

Chicago Grizzlies

On the Defense (Free Prequel)

Something like Hate

Something like Lust

Something like Love

The Nest

Mr. Heartbreaker

Mr. Broody

Mr. S (Title to be revealed)

Mr. C (Title to be revealed)

Holiday Romances

Single and Ready to Jingle

Claus and Effect

Merry Kissmas

Cockamamie Unicorn Ramblings

We're in shock that in the first three books in The Greene Family series, we managed to pull off three tropes we haven't written before. Well... if you're a fan than you know that Dom Mancini in Wild Steamy Hook-up was technically a Vegas wedding, but they weren't strangers when they got hitched. This was a true "I married a stranger in Vegas" story.

There wasn't a lot that changed in this book from what we initially had plotted except that when we were first conceptualizing the series, Logan was going to be a Rockstar, then an actor and in the end we went with him being an MMA Fighter. We wanted him to chase Nikki after they were married because who doesn't love a guy who pursues what he wants? His mom, Pauline was going to play a more central role in this story, but I think you know us well enough to know that she'll pop up in more Greene family books.

Nikki was a hard one to crack, we know, but sometimes those scars from childhood run deep. We're just glad in the end she trusted Logan like she should because that boy is head over heels in love with her!

Without our team you wouldn't have any of our books! Seriously, they take on a lot of the work so that we can write!

Danielle Sanchez and the entire Wildfire Marketing Solutions team.

Cassie from Joy Editing for line edits.

Ellie from My Brother's Editor for line edits.

My Brother's Editor for proofreading.

Hang Le for the cover and branding for the entire series.

Wander Aguiar for his awesome job of photographing our Nikki and Logan.

Bloggers who consistently carve out time to read, review and/or promote us.

Piper Rayne Unicorns who love our characters like as much as we do!

Readers who took the time to read our story when there's so many choices out there.

WHOA! What'd you think of that cliffhanger with Jed!?! I think we're just as excited as you to see how this all comes together.

xo,

Piper & Rayne

ABOUT PIPER & RAYNE

Piper Rayne is a USA Today Bestselling Author duo who write "heartwarming humor with a side of sizzle" about families, whether that be blood or found. They both have e-readers full of one-clickable books, they're married to husbands who drive them to drink, and they're both chauffeurs to their kids. Most of all, they love hot heroes and quirky heroines who make them laugh, and they hope you do, too!